MW00436681

SEALS

He moved to Sterne's body and pulled it back to lay it next to Boone. He then checked the dead VC and NVA, taking their weapons, searching their packs for extra grenades, finding a few ... Sterne and Boone could be used for a final ambush. Booby-trap them and take a few of the enemy out.

Quickly he rigged the bodies. He pulled the pins of the grenades and slipped them into position under the dead. As Charlie tried to move them, the safety spoons would fly, arming the grenades. Seconds later, they would explode!

TARGET!

Avon Books are available at special quantity discounts for bulk purchases for sales promotions, premiums, fund raising or educational use. Special books, or book excerpts, can also be created to fit specific needs.

For details write or telephone the office of the Director of Special Markets, Avon Books, Dept. FP, 105 Madison Avenue, New York, New York 10016, 212-481-5653.

STEVE MACKENZIE

AVON
PUBLISHERS OF BARD, CAMELOT, DISCUS AND FLARE BOOKS

SEALS #4: TARGET! is an original publication of Avon Books. This work has never before appeared in book form. This work is a novel. Any similarity to actual persons or events is purely coincidental.

AVON BOOKS
A division of
The Hearst Corporation
105 Madison Avenue
New York, New York 10016

Copyright © 1987 by Kevin D. Randle
Published by arrangement with the author
Library of Congress Catalog Card Number: 87-91595
ISBN: 0-380-75193-3

First Avon Printing: November 1987

AVON TRADEMARK REG. U.S. PAT. OFF. AND IN OTHER COUNTRIES. MARCA REGISTRADA. HECHO EN U.S.A.

Printed in the U.S.A.

K–R 10 9 8 7 6 5 4 3 2 1

1

Army Staff Sergeant Ronald Geist crouched among the bushes, palms, and grasses covering the ridge hidden fourteen klicks inside Laos. For two long, hot days, and seemingly longer nights, Geist and his four-man team had been stationed on the bluff that overlooked a well-used portion of the Ho Chi Minh Trail—a portion just visible through breaks and gaps in the vegetation and showing the trail to be more than a pathway through the jungle. It was a highway to the south. They had stayed there counting the traffic, the vehicles, the people, the weapons, and the bicycles. They had rarely spoken to each other, and then only in whispers into each other's ears that even the rest of the team couldn't hear. They had eaten cold C-rations, buried the cans when they finished, slept in shifts, and sipped water from one of the five canteens that each of them carried. None of them had moved more than ten feet from where they had established their camp even to relieve themselves, and the smell was beginning to permeate the area.

At midnight each night, Geist used the small radio,

a URC-10 that wasn't more than a survival radio, but since it was ultrahigh frequency, it had great range. For ten seconds, Geist broadcast a series of numbers— a code that told the operator at the other end that he and his patrol still lived and still observed.

On the third day, the last that they would be in the field overlooking the trail, Geist saw something that scared him. The nature of the traffic changed. No longer was it two or three men walking together, or steering a supply-laden bicycle, but large military units. Companies and battalions. Hundreds of men and women dressed in the dark green of the NVA escorting dozens of men and women wearing the black of the Viet Cong.

Geist used his binoculars, a shade cut from cardboard taped to the barrels of the lenses to keep the sun from reflecting from them, and studied the soldiers below him. Not the irregulars, guerrillas and part-time soldiers that marked the majority of the armies fielded by the enemy, but professionals who knew how to carry their equipment and how to use it, and who were apparently massing for the opportunity to attack the Americans and their South Vietnamese allies.

It was midafternoon when he decided that he had seen enough, more than enough. The VC and NVA had begun diverting from the trail, moving overland through the jungle, deeper into Laos. And the more he watched, the more of the enemy he had seen. He rolled to his right so that he could slip the binoculars back into their case. He snapped it shut, then wiped the sweat from his face and rubbed it on the front of his stained and dirty fatigue shirt.

Geist shifted slightly to the right and touched Corporal John Gibson on the shoulder. Gibson looked at Geist and raised a dark eyebrow in question.

"We go," said Geist. He hitchhiked a thumb over his shoulder to let Gibson know they were going to pull out to the east, back to Vietnam.

Gibson nodded, touched the man next to him. When each of them was ready, Geist moved to the rear, backing through the thick jungle growth, sliding his feet along slowly so that he didn't make any noise rattling leaves or scraping his boot on a bit of wood. He reached the two men stationed there, who had been guarding his back as he watched the trail, and let them know it was time to get out.

At that point each of the men got to his feet. Geist slipped a sweaty hand down the stock of his M-16 and felt the safety. He crouched, pulled his pack from the bush where he had hidden it, shouldered and shifted it until it sat comfortably on his back, and glanced at the other four men.

There was a sameness about them. Each dressed in tiger-striped jungle fatigues, uniforms that contained black stripes that helped them blend into the bright greens and black shadows of the jungle. The uniforms were stained with the white of salt rings from sweat that had evaporated in the night, and blackened with the dampness of the sweat from the new day. The men's faces showed a four- or five-day growth of beard, mixed with sweat and the grease of camo paint, giving each of them a wild look. None of them wore a steel pot, but each had a boonie hat. They wore go-to-hell rags that were sweat dark around their necks.

As they all gathered around Geist, each aware that he was pulling the patrol two days early, they heard him whisper, "As soon as we cross into Vietnam, I call for airlift."

They each nodded and Geist said, "Gibson, you're on the point. Back to Vietnam via direct."

Gibson turned and stepped around a giant teak tree, running a hand over its smooth trunk. He pushed the huge, broadleaves of a bush out of the way and moved off through the undergrowth, keeping to the shadows. He walked forward carefully, slowly, aware that the enemy was near and the slightest noise might give him away.

As they moved away from the bluff, from the break in the triple canopy jungle, the ground became wrapped in a perpetual twilight. Overhead were the interlocking leaves of the trees and bushes that effectively blocked out the sun and the rain and held in the heat and humidity. Within minutes it seemed that each of them was wrapped in the wet towels of a steambath. They sweated heavily, soaking their uniforms completely in moments.

They didn't hurry. It was more important not to make noise and not to leave signs of their passing. Through the thickness of the jungle, they moved only two hundred meters in an hour, but it was a tough two hundred meters. With the opressive heat and humidity and the strain of not making noise, they wore down quickly. Gibson crouched near a large bush, partially concealed in it, and waited for Geist to catch him. Each of the men dropped into the nearest cover, facing in opposite directions, searching for signs of pursuit, signs of the enemy.

As dusk came, it began to rain, but the water wasn't reaching the ground because the jungle canopy was too thick. The rain slid down, infiltrated onto the jungle floor by running from one broadleaf to the next, to the trunk of a tree, until it seeped into the ground. As the men brushed by the bushes, they got wet. It made the patrol more difficult, more miserable, because the water refused to evaporate.

At midnight they crossed the border into South Vietnam, but they didn't know it. There were no border checkpoints, there was no long fence, there was just more jungle. Geist halted them for an hour to let them rest and try to wipe some of the rain from their weapons and equipment.

Geist was about to get them up and moving when he heard a quiet sound near him. It wasn't the natural noise of the jungle, a small animal moving in the dark, but something that seemed to be human. Geist froze, waiting, listening. He stared into the darkness but could see nothing.

Geist lifted his right hand slowly and touched the hilt of the big Randall combat knife he had taped upside down on his shoulder harness, almost as if to reassure himself that it was still there. Then he reached down, feeling the hand grenades he had fastened to his pistol belt.

The noise had disappeared as quickly as it came. Geist wasn't sure what to do. He might have heard the VC moving into an ambush site. If that was true, they would probably remain until morning, at which time they were liable to see Geist and his men. And if Geist tried to move them earlier, the VC would probably spot them and open fire.

If it was the VC.

Geist rocked back on his heels, crouched in the dark jungle, shielded by a large bush. He listened but heard nothing else except the buzz of insects around him. Slowly he shifted to the right, toward Gibson, and touched the corporal on the shoulder. Gibson had to shove his face close to Geist just to see the hand signals.

Gibson began to move to the east again, slowly, carefully, setting each foot down cautiously, waiting for the snap of a twig or the crunch of a dry leaf. Geist was right behind him, no more than a foot or two, afraid that he would lose sight of Gibson in the dark. The rest of the patrol was strung out behind them, the last man holding onto the pistol belt of the man in front of him.

They worked their way through the jungle slowly, each man either holding onto the man in front, or walking within a foot of him so that he was a black outline in the black jungle. Geist had put out a hand to touch Gibson's shoulder when the point man tripped.

There was a grunt and Geist realized that the voice was not Gibson's. He reached out, grabbed a hairful of hair, and pulled. A hand wrapped around his wrist, and Geist grabbed it, jerking on it. There was resistance for an instant and then Geist was yanked forward, stumbling to his knees. He fell heavily, crushing a small thorny bush with a loud rattle of leaves and popping of branches.

As he fell, Geist grabbed at his knife, snapping it free. He dropped forward, pushing on the man there. Geist's face was only inches from that of the enemy. He knew it wasn't Gibson because of the breath. The man had been eating nouc-mam.

Geist shoved a hand up against the enemy soldier, his fingers collapsing the VC's nostrils, the heel of his hand forcing the chin up and back. With his right hand, Geist swiped from left to right, the blade of the knife slicing through the soft skin of the throat. There was a spurt of blood, the warm liquid washing over

Geist's hands as the man on the ground bucked, trying to free himself.

Geist leaned forward, throwing his weight against the man's shoulders, and rolled to the left slightly. He tried to slam the knife home, up under the rib cage, but the angle was wrong. He heard the blade grate against bone as the knife turned in his hand. He tried again, this time aiming at the kidney, driving it in deeply.

With ebbing strength, the VC reached up and tried to ram a thumb into Geist's eye, but the thumbnail only cut the skin along Geist's cheek. Geist collapsed then, his upper body against the head of the VC, holding him down as he bucked a last time. There was a gurgle in the throat and then nothing.

Geist rolled to the left, away from his victim. He stood, his back to a tree, and stared into the night. Around him he could hear the quiet stuggles of the men fighting with knives and hands, neither side sure of what they had stumbled into. Geist pulled a grenade from his pistol belt and jerked the pin free. He turned and lobbed the grenade into the jungle, dropping as he did. He knew that throwing a grenade without any idea of the terrain around him wasn't a good idea, but he didn't have a choice. He needed to break the contact so that they could get away before they were all killed.

As the grenade exploded with a loud, flat bang, a shape loomed out of the dark near him, and he could tell that it was another VC. The man was too short, too thin to be one of the Americans on the patrol. He wore the distinctive pith helmet favored by the Viet Cong. Geist grabbed him, yanked him close, and pushed the knife into the man's stomach, ripping upward. The man screamed, his voice high and strained, like tires on dry pavement. Geist heard the wet slapping as the intestines spilled. He used the knife again, trying to cut the man's throat to stop the screaming.

As the dead man dropped to the ground, Geist dodged to the right, away from the body. He slipped to one knee, his head up, listening, unable to see anything. There was a scream to his left that was cut off sharply, but Geist could see nothing in that direction.

Geist knew what he had to do. Orders had been explicit, especially with the information he had. A large buildup of enemy forces just a few klicks from the Vietnamese border, inside Laos. It meant that something was brewing, and he had a duty to communicate that information to his contacts. He had to move away from the fight even if it meant abandoning the men of his patrol. They had orders to do the same. In this situation, it was every man for himself. It wasn't a situation that Geist liked, but it was the one he found himself in.

Slowly he backed up until he felt the smoothness of a teak tree. He could feel the sweat on his face and body. Consciously he tried to slow his breathing. It had been rasping in his throat as if he had just sprinted four hundred meters. He wanted to wipe his face, drink from his canteen, but he was afraid that any unnecessary movement would give away his position.

At that moment there was a burst of automatic weapons fire. Geist could see the muzzle flashes sparkling against the black background. Green tracers looped through the jungle, disappearing with solid smacks as they hit trees, or ricocheting high to vanish in the triple canopy cover.

Geist watched as the firing stopped, heard the quiet clicks and snaps as the man tried to strip one magazine from his weapon to reload it. Geist took another grenade and threw it as hard as he could at the area where the muzzle flashes had been. He ducked down, turned his face away so that he wouldn't ruin his night vision in the flash of light when the grenade detonated.

As the grenade exploded, Geist was up again, moving now. He heard a scream pierce the jungle, a wail that rose and fell as if mimicking a police siren. There was a shout in Vietnamese and then the jungle seemed to erupt. A dozen AK-47s fired on full auto, their rounds ripping through the vegetation and slamming into the trees. An RPD joined in, raking the surrounding area with a sustained burst that scattered the green, glowing tracers in a full circle.

Geist fell to his hands and knees and then to his belly, easing himself forward. He heard the bark of an M-16 behind him and knew that whoever had fired would be dead in seconds. Grenades and knives protected the Americans in this kind of fight. The muzzle flashes of the M-16 would only identify their locations for the temporarily superior firepower of the VC. Too many enemy weapons had begun firing, and Geist knew that he was badly outnumbered.

Slowly he moved away from the fight, under bushes, around trees, keeping low. Behind him the firing increased, but he couldn't hear any American weapons involved. It was as if the VC were shooting at shadows and hadn't realized that no one was firing back.

He kept crawling forward, making almost no progress since he had to be quiet. The slightest noise would tip the VC. But he kept moving, thinking only about the task, about moving a hand and then a foot, setting it down slowly, quietly. He thought about getting into a rhythm that would take him through the jungle away from the ambush site, away from the battle, and away from his friends. Just get the rhythm going and keep it going until he was in the clear.

Once he had an almost irresistible urge to take a drink of water. Take out a canteen and empty it, but he couldn't risk it. He didn't know how far he had gotten from the enemy or what time it was because he couldn't see his watch. He wanted to keep going until it was dawn. All he could do was keep moving, waiting for signs that the night was nearly over.

Dawn came abruptly. A thousand monkeys suddenly started shouting at one another, announcing the sunrise to the rest of the jungle. They were joined by birds that lived in the top of the canopy, and the noise from them filled the jungle so that even the roar of jets high overhead was lost.

As the ground began to lighten so that Geist could see the trees, the bushes, the obstacles, he got to his feet. He used the covering noise of the monkeys and birds to rush forward, putting distance between himself and the enemy. He hurried, using a quick compass reference to make sure that he hadn't gotten turned around in the night. To make sure that he wasn't running back into Laos. To make sure that he was heading for the rally point that he and his men had agreed on before they had started the mission.

The noise died as abruptly as it started. It was as if someone had thrown a switch. Geist dropped to the ground then, breathing through his mouth, trying to get his second wind. The jungle still had a steambath quality. He rolled to the right and sat up next to the rough bark of a palm tree. Geist drained one of his canteens, the water warm and tasting of plastic. He sat for a moment, resting, his eyes burning from lack of sleep, his body itching from its coating of dirt and sweat. He took out his map, a rubberized chart that wouldn't disintegrate in the humidity of the jungle, and studied it. As near as he could tell, he was four or five klicks from the RP, a high area where a single helicopter could land or drop a jungle penetrator if necessary. Once there, he would be only a couple of minutes from his camp. Only a couple of seconds from safety. If he could get through the last bit of jungle.

Geist forced himself to his feet, tired from a night of crawling through the jungle and from the days of forced inactivity as he had watched the traffic on the Ho Chi Minh Trail. He moved carefully, stiffly, working his way down one hillside and up another to the RP. Around him there was nothing but the jungle, the animals and insects that lived in it, and the heat and humidity.

It was late in the afternoon when he finally found the clearing that was the rally point. He stayed in the trees, watching the area and the surrounding jungle, but saw nothing to indicate that any of the others had reached it. And he saw nothing to indicate that the VC had set up an ambush around it. With so few landing spots in the area, the VC sometimes set ambushes around the most likely ones, hoping to luck into something.

Geist took the URC-10 from his pack and made a radio call. He used the code that established him as the real Sergeant Geist, because Charlie sometimes got on the radio to mimic Americans. They were sometimes able to draw in helicopters with their fake requests for assistance. Once the calls were made,

Geist couldn't do anything, so he waited—waited for his men to arrive, and waited for the helicopter.

In thirty minutes the helicopter, accompanied by two gunships, buzzed the clearing, turned, and hovered down, landing in the bright afternoon sun. Geist sprinted out of the trees, dived into the cargo compartment, and hung on as the pilot jerked in an armload of pitch, climbing out before anyone knew he had been there.

Geist turned and looked out the cargo compartment door but saw nothing on the ground to indicate that any of the others had made the rally point. He was alone. He sat on the troop seat, fastened the seat belt, and then stared at the floor. He wasn't aware of the rush-colored stains on his right sleeve, the right side of his fatigue jacket, and his right trouser leg. He wasn't aware of how dirty he was or how he smelled. He only knew that only he had gotten on the chopper at the rally point and that the rest of his men had been left somewhere in the jungle. He hoped that the information he had was worth the sacrifice.

2

Lieutenant Mark Tynan sat in the noisy, smoke-filled club on what was to be the last night of his incountry R and R, watching the two Vietnamese girls and one Australian go-go dancing at the ends of the bar and on a raised stage behind it. He was wearing jungle fatigues, new ones that had been starched and ironed but that had wilted in the humidity of the afternoon. There was no insignia on his uniform, other than a single patch above the left breast pocket that said "U.S. Navy."

Sitting next to him, where she could see only one of the dancers but could look out into the filled room, was Bobbi Harris. She was an employee of the American Embassy in Saigon. She was a brown-haired woman, tall and slender, with bright blue eyes. She was watching the one Vietnamese girl who was moving about twice as fast as the music was playing. She had already stripped off the miniature top of her bikini, throwing it into the crowd. Her long, black hair was whipping around, and the light coating of sweat on her body made it glow in the dim light from the recessed ceiling lamps.

Harris leaned an elbow on the corner of the table and nearly shouted over the pounding of the rock music. "I couldn't do that."

"What? Dance or take off your clothes in public?" Tynan yelled back.

"Dance," she said, grinning. "She's been dancing like that for almost an hour. I'd die from the heat."

Tynan looked at her closely and saw the beads of sweat on her forehead and along her upper lip. "Yeah," he called back. "I see what you mean."

She reached out and took his hand, squeezing it gently. "You want to stay here? We could go somewhere else. Like my apartment."

"We could," said Tynan, brushing at the sweat on his forehead with the sleeve of his uniform, "except I promised a couple of my men we would meet them here this evening." He saw the look on her face and smiled. "And then we can go to your apartment. They just want the chance to buy their skipper a beer, and I've managed to duck them for forty-eight hours."

"Okay," she said slyly. She leaned back in her chair and pulled the sweat-damp blouse away from her skin. She blew down the front to cool herself and then looked at Tynan out of the corners of her eyes, a trace of a smile on her lips. She saw that he was watching closely.

A moment later Tynan stood and waved at two men who had entered the crowded bar and stood at the door surveying the nearly two hundred Americans in the place. Tynan caught their attention finally and watched as they moved toward him, dodging around the other GIs.

When they were close, the older of the two yelled, "I should have known that our skipper would be here with the prettiest lady in the bunch." He smiled at her and asked, "You don't mind if I say that, do you?"

"Of course not." She laughed. "Keep it up. Flattery will get you everywhere."

The man hooked a chair with his foot, dragging it close, and sat down next to Harris, staring into her eyes. He took her hand, smiled broadly, and said, "I'm Chief Petty Officer Russel Vaughan, and I believe that I have fallen in love for the first time today."

"Well, Russel," said Harris, "I'm afraid that you're going to be disappointed."

"In that case I will drink," he said, standing up so that he could flag down one of the waitresses. Her hair was sweat-damp and her light blouse clung to her body as if it had been molded on. Russel smiled and said, "Ba Muoi Ba." He pointed to the other man and added, "One for each of us."

As the waitress hurried off, Tynan said, "The quiet one is Thomas Jones. You should remember him because you met him when we were on the ship in the Atlantic."

Harris nodded and smiled. "Of course I remember." She tugged on Tynan's hand. "Can we go now?"

"Ah, Skipper," said Russel, "if you have other plans, Tom and I can make our own fun."

"I have the time to drink a beer with you," said Tynan. He glanced at Harris and then added, "But it will have to be a quick one. A very quick one."

"Well, now, Skipper," yelled Russel as the music seemed to get louder, "I would think that time spent with the lady would be more beneficial than time swapped with sailors. That is to say, more fun could be had, if you take my meaning, sir.''

Tynan rubbed a hand over his face, wiping away the sweat. The temperature in the bar had climbed significantly as more men entered it. The cloud of blue cigarette smoke seemed to grow thicker and burned his eyes. He stared at Russel and knew that there was no diplomatic way to get out. Russel was telling him to take Bobbi off and have fun with her. So, following Russel's suggestion, Tynan and Harris took off and strolled down Tu Do Street and circled over a couple of blocks to find themselves on Le Loi Street. There were a dozen clubs on it. Music, from country and western to rock and roll, blared from the open doors and, in one case, a broken front window. The streets were brightly lighted, as if no one knew that there was a war on and those who did didn't care.

The streets were packed with vehicles—motor scooters ridden by young women in short skirts, lambrettas carrying half a dozen passengers each, beat-up old taxis, busses, jeeps, and military trucks, and even a couple of limousines. Tynan stood on a corner and watched the swirling traffic and the pedestrian tide and wondered about a country that could be at war—a war that often came to the center of the city—and seem to ignore it so well. Maybe it was a case of making money while there was time because no one knew how long it would last. Someday all the Americans, with all their riches, would be gone, leaving the locals to find a new way to make some money.

Harris sensed the change in Tynan, a shift from a lighthearted mood to one of depression. She took his hand and pressed it against her hip. She tried to flag down a taxi to take them back to her apartment. "Something wrong?" she asked.

Tynan looked at two young Vietnamese girls standing next to the door of a bar, their skirts so short that they looked more like wide belts. They both wore tight blouses with the tails knotted just under their small breasts, displaying their flat, dark bellies.

"No," he said, smiling, suppressing his urge to tell her that there was something inherently wrong with the system that spawned this nightmare, this parody of the wealth of the United States. These were thoughts that were too heavy for a last night on the town with one of the few American women in Vietnam.

"No," he repeated, shaking himself. He took her hand, smiled, and said, "You mentioned your apartment. If it's air-conditioned, and you have ice . . ."

"It's air-conditioned, but I don't know how cool it will be. The power is so unreliable that you can never tell."

A taxi, an old Ford that might have been red once, pulled to the curb, and Tynan jerked open the rear door. Harris climbed in, slid halfway across the seat, and then waited. Tynan followed and let her lean against his shoulder as she gave the driver her address.

A few minutes later they pulled up to one of the major hotels in Saigon where the American civilians lived. Some were reporters covering the war, some were embassy employees, and some were civilian contractors working for the U.S. Army. Tynan tossed a couple of bills of MPC—the military paper that was used in Vietnam instead of greenbacks—at the driver and hurried after Harris. She had stopped at the top of the three steps that led into the hotel to wait for him.

Together they went upstairs, ignoring the intermittent elevator. Harris unlocked her door and pushed it open. Tynan entered, turned, and waited. Harris closed the door, locked it, and moved to Tynan. For a moment they stood together, hugging, and then Harris broke away, stepping deeper into the dark, cool, room. She turned on a single, dim lamp so that there was a little light.

"So," she said.

Tynan moved forward and sat on the edge of the bed, looking at her, at her sweat-damp clothes that hadn't begun to dry in the coolness of the apartment. "So," he repeated.

She reached up and slowly began to unbutton her blouse, tilting her head forward so that she could watch herself. She shrugged her shoulders, and the blouse slipped to the floor. She turned slightly, tugged at the zipper on the side of her skirt, and rolled the skirt over her hips so that it fell away. She stood in front of Tynan in only her panties and bra and a light coating of sweat that was rapidly drying.

Tynan got up and moved to her. He reached behind her and unsnapped her bra. He pulled her close, and kissed her ear and then her mouth as she molded herself to him.

The next morning, Tynan caught a chopper to Nha Be, the naval base that was southeast of Saigon and situated on a river delta not far from the South China Sea. They landed on what looked like a dock which ran out into the widening river. There were two other choppers parked there, but neither of them belonged to the Navy. One was Army and had a dozen patches over bullet holes, and the other was Air Force, looking as if it had just come from the factory.

Tynan climbed out the of the cargo compartment of the Huey and stared into the distance. Not far way, down a gravel road lined with whitewashed stones, he could see a low, flat, gray building. He leaned back in, retrieved his pack that included his weapon, a CAR-15, and then straightened. As he stepped away, the helicopter took off in a swirling cloud of red dust and whipping debris. In seconds it was gone, and with it most of the noise, leaving Tynan wrapped in silence.

He walked down the road, past a Navy staff car, the engine idling and the windows rolled up. He passed a dozen buildings, all painted gray, without the sandbags that would have surrounded the structures on an Army or Air Force base. Past the dining hall that had real curtains in the windows, he turned again until he came to a nondescript building that housed the intelligence office. He opened the single door and entered. The cool breeze from the air conditioning hit with the force of a physical slap. He walked down the narrow hallway, past closed doors that weren't labeled, until he found the one he wanted.

Inside, a clerk sat behind a single metal desk that had seen better days. A couple of mismatched chairs to one side flanked a low table containing newspapers and magazines. A couple of watercolors and a couple of captured weapons were displayed on the paneled walls. A ceiling fan turned lazily overhead.

The clerk stopped typing and said, ''Yes?''

''Commander Walker is expecting me.''

The clerk turned back to his typing and said, ''Go right in then.''

Tynan opened the door and stepped into the inner office. He saw that he was the last to arrive. Russel and Jones sat in two metal folding chairs set against the far wall. Sitting in the two chairs reserved for visitors were the two other men who were regular members of Tynan's team. Sterne and Boone looked up and acknowledged their skipper.

Commander Walker sat behind his desk, holding a yellow pencil in both hands, waiting patiently. He waved the pencil and said, "We can start now. Mark, put your weapon in the corner with the others."

Tynan nodded but didn't move.

Sterne got to his feet and said, "Take my seat, Skipper. I feel like standing."

Tynan set his weapon in the corner and then sat in the chair that Sterne had vacated. He glanced over his shoulder at the other men, nodded to them, and then turned his attention back to Walker.

"All right," said Walker, "let's get this show on the road." He got up and moved to the door. He told the clerk that he didn't want to be disturbed for any reason, then shut and locked the door. Next he lowered the blinds, fiddling with the strings until he had them turned so that no one could see in. When he had everything set just the way he wanted it, he sat behind his desk again and said, "Gentlemen, this is Sergeant Ronald Geist of the Army's Special Forces. He has spent the last few days watching the Ho Chi Minh Trail. Sergeant, why don't you let us in on what you saw."

Geist stood up and looked at the gathered men. He shifted his feet nervously, cleared his throat, and said, "I spent a couple of days watching the traffic on the trail and I can tell you, the nature of it changed. Changed radically."

He spent twenty minutes talking about the radical changes, what he had seen, and what he had experienced. He explained that the nature of the information was such that he had left the rest of his team in the field to make sure that his intelligence was reported.

As Geist sat back down, Walker asked, "Anybody have any questions?"

"Just one," said Tynan. "This been confirmed?"

"By confirmed," said Walker, "I assume you mean corroborated. The answer is yes. There have been other reports of a buildup in the general location investigated by Sergeant Geist as well as other spotting teams, electronic surveillance and humint resources."

Tynan had to smile. "Humint resources? You mean some VC told you something?"

Walker shot a look at Geist as if he wasn't to be trusted now that he had shared his intelligence with the Navy.

"Hey, listen," said Geist, "you people want to talk about this without me sitting around, I can go find a beer. In fact, I prefer beers to meetings."

"Well Sergeant . . ." began Walker.

"Shit," said Tynan. "I'm sure the sergeant is cleared to hear anything we might say."

Walker stood up. "Sergeant, if you would excuse us for a couple of minutes, there are some things that I need to discuss with Lieutenant Tynan and his team. Navy business. Then we'll probably need to see you again." He grinned and said, "So you won't be able to find that beer. Besides, it seems a bit early to be drinking."

"It's late enough somewhere," said Geist. He left quickly, shutting the door behind him.

As soon as Geist was gone, Walker said, "The feeling at all levels is that we cannot allow the buildup to continue. An analysis of the information from a dozen teams like Geist's, and all the other sources, including some electronic surveillance run by our own intelligence people, suggests that the VC and NVA are preparing to launch a large-scale offensive. Maybe something on the order of Tet of 1968. It could even be bigger than that.''

"And?" said Tynan.

"And it would not be the best time for such an offensive," said Walker. "There's pressure at home to end the war, or rather our involvement in it. Politically it wouldn't be a good time. Not with the elections coming up. A delay of six months would be better."

"A delay?" asked Tynan. "Why not just bomb the fuckers into the stone age, as the folks in Washington are fond of saying all the time."

Walker looked at the men sitting in the office, his eyes slipping from one to the next. "Tynan, I shouldn't have to explain overall strategies to you. And I shouldn't explain them in front of everyone."

"They won't tell," said Tynan.

"No, I suppose they won't," agreed Walker. "The idea is that we can't use our Air Force to hit these targets in Laos and Cambodia. They are dug in and spread out. Oh, saturation bombing would probably take care of it, given all the resources that we have at our disposal, but then we have problems at home. Students in the street are protesting our expansion of the war and disregarding the fact that the enemy has been operating there for years—protesting our inhumane actions by dropping all those bombs. The Administration doesn't need that right now—will not tolerate that right now because of the possible effects on the election."

"I can understand that," said Tynan slowly. "I don't like conducting the war in a certain way because a bunch of misinformed students might riot, or CBS News won't like it, but I can understand it. Understand while I watch men die because of aid and comfort provided by those students."

"Secondly," said Walker, ignoring what Tynan was saying, "no one wants to prevent the attacks forever. We want the NVA to come out and fight. During Tet we kicked their ass, and the feeling is that in a stand-up fight we could do it again. But we don't want that fight right now."

"Why not?" asked Tynan.

"The media," said Walker. "Look at Tet of '68. A complete victory for our side, but the press reported it as a loss. Then, when they figured out that Charlie had been destroyed, they tried to save face by claiming a psychological victory for the VC. Of course it wasn't one until they made it one, but I digress. We want them to launch their assault, we just don't like the timing."

"That," said Tynan reluctantly, "is something I can understand too." He thought of men fighting and dying so that politicians could keep jobs that they probably didn't deserve. He thought about men trading their lives for the convenience of men in Washington. It all made his blood run cold, but he knew that it was something that had gone on for centuries. And if he refused to do it, he would be court-martialed, probably dismissed from the service, and then someone less qualified would be given the job. "Where do we come in?" he asked.

"Army SOG, that is, the Studies and Observations Group, has asked that you be deployed to help out. Missions on the other side of the border. Low-key, quick. In and out. No muss and no media attention."

"You mean that we have a real choice on this one?" said Tynan.

Walker stopped talking and rested both elbows on his desk. He touched his fingers to his lips. Finally he said, "Not really. You and your team have been temporarily transferred to MACV-SOG. Sergeant Geist is going to be your liaison."

"Wait just a minute," said Tynan.

"No," answered Walker. "Orders have been cut. The plans are in place. Briefings will be conducted and targets assigned in the next twelve hours. You should be in the field inside of twenty-four hours."

3

Within thirty minutes of completing his interview with Walker, Tynan found himself, along with his team members and Sergeant Geist, on a Huey heading back to Saigon. Tynan sat on the red troop seat, his head against the gray soundproofing, listening to the heavy beat of the rotors and the roaring whine of the turbine. He tried to concentrate on his evening with Harris, tried to remember the feel of her sweat-damp skin as he slid her red bikini panties down her thighs, but Commander Walker and his briefing kept intruding unwanted. Walker had never actually told him what the mission was supposed to be. He had just kept repeating that it was something that the men at MACV-SOG had designed.

Tynan, as a Navy SEAL, had heard of MACV-SOG, but had never worked with it. Walker explained that it stood for the MACV Studies and Observations Group, but would say no more about it. It might have been that he knew no more about it. Tynan suspected that it was a CIA operation that used the Army's Special Forces among others as its assets, but said nothing to Walker about it. Such things just weren't discussed. Everyone ignored it like it was a venereal disease. At any rate, in a few minutes, he would know more than he cared to about it.

They approached Saigon from the southeast, but rather than turning west to land at Tan Son Nhut, they skirted the east side of the city. Tynan saw just how sprawling it was—a large flat place of massive, beautiful buildings and ramshackle, makeshift hootches.

Finally they turned west and descended, landing on a rooftop heliport. Tynan wasn't sure what the next move was supposed to be, but as he stepped from the chopper, he was met by a Marine dressed in starched jungle fatigues.

"If you will follow me," the Marine said, "I will see that you get a lift to Cholon."

"Cholon?" said Tynan. "What the fuck is happening in Cholon?"

"Yes, sir," said the Marine. "I'm sure that I don't know what it's about, but there is a jeep and a deuce-and-a-half downstairs waiting for you and your men."

As the rest of the team climbed out of the helicopter, the Marine moved to a square white building, opened a metal door, and turned. "Would the last man through please make sure the door latches."

They made their way down a set of cement steps with steel protection on the front edges. The walls were bare and white, and it looked as if the stairway had not yet been finished. The Marine opened a door and led them into a hallway. The contrast was amazing. There was thick carpeting on the floor, textured wallpaper in dark browns trimmed with tan, oil paintings, and small tables spaced evenly along the walls. At the far end was a bank of elevators.

The Marine pushed a button and stepped back to wait. He smiled at the men but said nothing to them. When the elevator arrived, he let them enter first and then got on, pushing the button for the ground floor.

When the doors opened, the Marine led them out through a double set of glass doors and down a set of steps that were flanked by large, green bushes. He pointed to the jeep and truck sitting on the pavement several yards from the door. He put a hand up to block the bright sun and said, ''There's your ride. Drivers know where you're going.''

Tynan turned and waved at his men. ''Load your gear and climb on board.'' He tossed his pack in the back of the jeep, set his weapon there, and then got into the passenger's seat. He glanced at the driver, a young man with blond hair. He was wearing staff sergeant stripes and a green beret.

Without a word the sergeant twisted the ignition on the jeep and the engine roared to life. He shifted into first, grinding the gears as he fought the knob. He finally jammed it home, popped the clutch, and shot forward.

They exited through two high, wrought-iron gates that were anchored to thick stone pillars. There were pockmarks on one of them, as though it had been hit by machine-gun fire. Guard stations on both sides were manned by Marines wearing flak jackets and carrying M-16s. They turned into the street and headed toward Cholon.

Cholon was the Chinese section of Saigon, but as they entered the district, Tynan couldn't see anything different about it. Maybe it was just that he was unfamiliar with Saigon, and the variations between its sections were not immediately obvious. It did seem that the streets were relatively uncongested and clean. Of course, Tynan had seen some parts of Saigon, away from the glitter and chaos of the Tu Do Street area, that were cleaner and less congested. And there were sections on the outskirts, where people lived in cardboard boxes and cement conduits, that were dirtier and more crowded.

Finally they stopped in front of a small building that was almost indistinguishable from all the others except that it had no windows anymore. At one time there had been windows, but they had been bricked up and painted over. Tynan rocked back in his seat and stared upward. The building was three stories and the windows on the upper two floors were gone too. He thought that he could see a hint of radio antennas on the top, but the angle was wrong for him to be sure.

The Green Beret bent down and picked up a length of chain bolted to the floor at one end. He looped the chain through the steering wheel and used a padlock to secure it. The Army jeeps didn't have a key-activated ignition, so anyone could get in and start it. The chain prevented the steering wheel from turning.

He got out of the jeep, walked around the front, and waited on the sidewalk while Tynan grabbed his pack and weapon. As they stepped to the front door, the rest of Tynan's team dropped from the back of the deuce-and-a-half. They assembled on the sidewalk, the packs, equipment, and weapons forming a pile that nearly blocked traffic.

The Green Beret banged on the door and waited. A tinny voice from a speaker recessed to the side asked a question that Tynan couldn't hear. A moment later there was a loud buzz, and the sergeant grabbed the skinny handle, opening the steel-reinforced door.

"Inside," he said. "Down the hall and second

door on the right. You'll meet with Mr. Smith from Washington. He'll brief you and answer your questions."

"You're not going in with us?" asked Tynan.

"No, sir. I'm just the driver on this."

Tynan looked around at his men and said, "Let's move our gear inside." He watched as they shouldered it and then said to the sergeant, "Thanks for your help."

"Yes, sir."

Tynan entered the building. The dimly lit hallway was lined with doors made of reinforced steel. In the center of each door was a small peephole that looked more like a gunport. Tynan moved down the hall and took the knob on the second one on the right, but it wouldn't turn. He banged on the door. It echoed hollowly. The peephole popped open. Bright light blazed through the hole.

Tynan waited, but no one spoke on the other side and he wasn't sure that anyone was in there. Finally Tynan said, "I'm supposed to see Mr. Smith. From Washington?"

There was no talk from inside. Tynan heard a snap as a lock was taken off and the door opened. A man dressed in starched and pressed jungle fatigues, but with no insignia on them, stepped back, out of the way.

"Gentlemen," said a male voice on the right. "Please drop your gear and follow me. Weapons too. We'll take good care of them."

Tynan set his pack on the seat of a chair and leaned his CAR-15 against the arm. He saw that the room was painted white. There were four banks of lights on the ceiling. A single desk was shoved into the corner with a woman sitting behind it, typing.

She paid no attention to the people gathering. There was nothing on the walls or floor and only a couple of chairs.

The man who had spoken stepped to another door and opened it. Tynan followed and saw that it led into a theater—an impressive contrast. Dark woods paneled the walls; thick carpeting led down to the plush, theaterlike seats. There was a raised stage in one corner with an American flag set behind the podium. Near the podium was a small wooden table that held a water pitcher and several glasses. A single spotlight picked up the highlights of the dark woods and carpeting on the stage. There was a screen on the back wall, and projected on it was the CIA insignia.

The man walked to the stage and then turned. "Gentlemen, please be seated and I'll get started."

Tynan stopped about halfway down the aisle and said, "I was supposed to talk to Mr. Smith."

The man looked up from the notes he was studying on the podium. He looked at the men, watching them closely. "I'm Smith," he said. "Please, be seated."

When the men had taken their places, the theater dimmed and the spot focused on Smith vanished. The slide dissolved slowly, becoming bright red. A single word, in bright white, filled the screen. "Secret."

"Gentlemen," began Smith. "The contents of this briefing are classified as Secret, and any discussion of the contents outside this room is punishable by a ten-year prison term and a ten thousand-dollar fine."

The Secret slide winked out and was replaced by a map of Southeast Asia. Smith then told them about the buildup of enemy forces on the Laos and Cambodian sides of the border. He went into the political aspects, the timing of the buildup, and the American media.

Tynan was bored. He had listened to all that in Walker's office. In fact, given the speed with which Walker had wanted to act, sitting in Cholon listening to the same thing again seemed to be defeating the purpose.

The slide switched. The new one showed part of the Two Corps Tactical Zone. Centered was the small town of Dak To. Smith announced, "Special Forces Camp A-314 is based here along Highway Fourteen. It is near a fork in the road. One branch leads back into Laos and the other north eventually to Hoi An, where it meets Highway One just south of Da Nang. A fairly important, strategic location."

Smith flipped a page of his notes and said, "Information is that the NVA and the VC are building a strike force in that area. If they penetrate into South Vietnam, that camp and the fork it controls become very important. We want to stop them from launching their assault."

Now Tynan was alert. He glanced at the men who had come in with him. Sterne and Boone sat in the back looking as if they were about to go to sleep. Jones sat on the aisle, his eyes wide, trying to look interested. Russel sat by himself, staring at the floor. Geist also sat by himself, his eyes on Smith. He didn't seem to be paying attention. But then, Tynan guessed that Geist knew all this and had probably contributed some of the information to the briefing.

Smith said, "In the next week, we want you to move into the area and remove the leadership of the assault."

"Just how do we do that?" shouted Sterne from the back, apparently waking up.

The slides changed rapidly, showing a variety of men in a variety of uniforms. As the sequence progressed, Smith said, "These show the rank insignia of the NVA officers. You can see the differences in the uniforms, the badges of rank in them. The officers all carry sidearms. It'll give you a clue about who is important."

"Let me get this straight," said Tynan. "You want us to assassinate the officers."

Smith straightened out his papers and turned off the tiny light on the podium. "Well, we don't like the word *assassinate* around here, but that is essentially what we want. The feeling is, if we can take out the leadership, the assault will fail. They'll pull back for a while. Politically that is all that we want."

"I don't know," said Tynan. "This doesn't seem right."

"Look," said Smith, "we have hunter-killer teams out all over South Vietnam. We've even sent them into North Vietnam. Their jobs are to disrupt the enemy, and that is what they do. They just use a rifle at long distance. What difference does it make if we call in artillery on an enemy unit to kill randomly, or just pick off a couple of chosen targets to prevent a large-scale attack? All the same. And the victims are just as dead and we don't have to risk several units of our soldiers to kill those men."

Tynan rubbed his face. He thought about the changing nature of warfare and how war was being conducted in the modern world. He wanted to say that he didn't like ambushes because they didn't seem fair, but he knew the value of them. He didn't like bombing because the destruction couldn't be controlled. Some of the bombs always were long or short and destroyed buildings or killed people who shouldn't have been targeted. War should be fought by two armies in their brightly colored uniforms with strict rules. That didn't happen, and the innocent often got in the way. Maybe it was better that Tynan take a team into Laos and shoot the NVA officers.

While Tynan considered that, Smith went on to detail exactly what had been observed, some of the troop locations, and where Tynan could expect to have the best luck. There were maps that showed it, and photos—most fuzzy and taken with telephoto lenses—that showed some of the more important NVA officers. Finally Smith wound down. He stood at the podium, waiting for one of the men to say something.

"We'll need some special equipment," said Tynan, realizing that he had no choice. This wasn't a briefing being conducted to get his opinion, but one being held so that he would have all the information he needed to complete his task.

"That's no problem. You'll find everything you need at the air base. You'll be flying out of Bien Hoa, since it is strictly a military installation and we can control access to it. We can keep the media at arm's length."

Tynan turned and looked at Sterne. He figured that either Sterne or Boone, or maybe both of them, would be shooting the enemy soldiers. Both of them were excellent marksmen, and both had killed before. That meant he didn't have to worry about either of them freezing with a finger on the trigger and the target in the sights.

Sterne understood what Tynan's look meant. He said, "Since we don't have the weapons on hand, I'll need an opportunity to zero them."

"That's the purpose of going into Ban Me Thuot. You'll have a chance to zero the weapon and check the local intel reports with the Special Forces A Detachment stationed there. They have been alerted."

Tynan turned in his seat again and looked at his men. None of them seemed to want to ask anything. Sterne had been told that he would be allowed to zero his weapon, so he was happy. Tynan couldn't help feeling that he was being tossed into a situation without benefit of all the information available, but then it wouldn't be the first time that it happened.

"If there are no other questions," said Smith, "I'll see that you have transport to Bien Hoa." He waited for a moment and then added, "Oh, if the situation should arise and you could capture one of these guys, I think that would be greatly appreciated."

That was too much. Tynan slumped back in his chair. "You're not serious."

Smith slowly folded his notes and put them in the side pocket of his fatigues. He stepped down from the stage and looked directly at Tynan. "I'm very serious. I mentioned it only because there are some intelligence types that would welcome the opportunity to interrogate a sampling of the field leadership of the NVA." He smiled slyly. "Maybe give them the opportunity to experience the questioning that our boys are undergoing up in Hanoi. Turnabout is fair play."

"We'll do what we can," said Tynan tiredly.

"That's all that we ask." Smith stopped and held out a hand, gesturing at the door. "Let's vacate the area. We'll get you to Bien Hoa so that you can catch your flight to Ban Me Thuot."

4

They caught a C-123 flown by pilots with the 90th Special Operations Wing. The plane, which had almost no markings, took off from Bien Hoa late in the afternoon, climbed out to the west, and then turned to the north. Tynan sat strapped into the red webbing, his gear stored in the rear of the plane, and read a science-fiction novel. He should have been reading any of a dozen military manuals or unclassified reports, especially those that described the uniforms and rank insignia of the NVA and the VC, but he just wasn't in the mood.

Of course, he hadn't been in the mood when Mr. Smith from Washingtion had taken him aside, away from his men, and said, "There is one other thing that I want you to know, but I don't want the information spread too far. You may need to know, but I don't want you to pass the information along."

Great, thought Tynan. That was exactly what he needed.

Smith pulled a small map out of his pocket and opened it. He lowered his voice and said, "There are a couple of villages in the area that we're supplying. That means we are offering military aid and training to help them fight the Pathet Lao and other communist sympathizers. If you get into trouble on the other side of the border, these are villages where you can expect to get some help. It means that you don't have to get back into South Vietnam for help.''

Tynan took the map and studied it. Most of the villages were close to the border.

''One thing,'' added Smith. ''You are not to go there unless it is an extreme emergency. We don't want these places compromised. We don't want the information to get out because then there would be political pressure to end our support.''

''Why not use them to stop this buildup?'' asked Tynan. ''Keep it an all-Laos operation.''

''Because we don't want this compromised,'' said Smith again. ''Besides, these are not combat soldiers but irregulars. We want someone who is well trained and disciplined.''

Tynan started to fold the map, but Smith stopped him. ''You'll have to remember the villages. That map stays here.''

''There any code words I should know?'' asked Tynan.

''None that would be of use to you. If you have to go into the village you'll have to play it by ear.''

''Great,'' said Tynan.

Again he forced his mind from the meeting and looked at the men in the airplane with him. Across the fuselage from him, Sterne was sleeping, his head back against the webbing, his mouth open. Boone sat next to Sterne, chain-smoking cigarettes, a small, red butt can in his left hand, his elbows on his knees, and his eyes on the deck. Neither man seemed to have a care in the world. Geist was in the back talking to the loadmaster, who was sitting on a pile of equipment.

Jones had lain down on the troop seat, pulled his hat over his eyes, and gone to sleep immediately. He hadn't been interested in anything that anyone had to say. He only wanted to sleep.

Tynan turned his attention back to his novel. He read a page but remembered none of it. The briefing kept intruding. In fact, he wasn't having much luck concentrating on anything but the briefings. Finally he closed the book and let the thoughts wash over him.

Actually, the mission wasn't that unusual. A patrol into suspected enemy territory. The difference was that he was taking his men into Laos instead of South Vietnam to shoot enemy officers instead of gathering information. Not deep into the swamps or jungles of Vietnam to ambush the VC.

He closed his eyes and listened to the vibrations of the twin engines of the C-123. He let his mind go, no longer concerned with moral ramifications of his orders. There really wasn't much difference in running an ambush and picking off the officers so that they couldn't lead an attack. He decided that fighting a war meant fighting a war.

Finally the loadmaster told them all to sit down and fasten their seat belts. The loadmaster woke up Jones and then moved to the back of the plane, checked the tie-downs, and then sat down himself. In minutes they were on the ground, taxiing toward the tower.

As the roar from the engines died and the ramp lowered, a man got on and moved directly to Tynan. He was a tall man wearing freshly starched fatigues that had stains under the arms and down the front. He had thick black hair that was obvious under his regulation Army baseball cap. There was a shadow on his chin that suggested he needed to shave again, and his eyebrows were so thick that they nearly touched over his nose.

"Are you Lieutenant Tynan?" he asked.

"Yes," said Tynan. "What can I do for you?"

The man checked a page on the clipboard he carried and then looked at the men in the plane. He could easily separate the flight crew from the passengers, since none of the passengers wore earphones. He seemed to study each of the men, as if his list provided clues about them. Finally he said, "Please gather your equipment and come with me."

The man turned and stepped down the ramp. Tynan looked at his men, shrugged, and then picked up his equipment, shouldering his rifle. He followed the man down the ramp, put a hand to his eyes to block the bright afternoon sun, and hoped that he wouldn't have to walk far. They had gone from the cool, dark interior of the plane to the bright, hot exterior of Ban Me Thuot in a matter of seconds, and the climatic changes were making him slightly sick.

The man had stopped by a jeep. He pointed to the passenger's side and then a second jeep behind it with an Army enlisted man sitting behind the wheel. "Your men can ride back there. One of them can ride up here with us. We'll escort you over to your quarters."

Tynan moved to the other side of the lead jeep but didn't make a move to either put his gear in it or climb in himself. "Before we surrender ourselves to you," said Tynan, "would you be kind enough to tell me just who the hell you are?"

"Oh, sorry. They called me about twenty minutes

ago and said for me to grab a couple of jeeps, get the special compound ready, and to get out here to meet the plane.'' He smiled and held out a hand. ''Name's Belcher. Army Special Forces. First lieutenant.'' He glanced at Tynan's Navy insignia and added, ''That's lieutenant j.g. to you.''

Tynan set his pack in the back and put his rifle in on top of it. He turned and yelled, ''Sterne, why don't you ride up here with me. The rest of you climb in that jeep.'' Tynan sat down, put a foot up on the dashboard, and said, ''Okay, James, take me home now.''

Belcher started the engine, jammed the gear lever forward, missed, tried again, ground them, and then popped the clutch. They lurched off the field in a cloud of red dust. Tynan looked back over his shoulder and saw the second jeep right behind them. Boone and Jones were sitting up on the sides in the back and were hanging on tight but looked as if they were going to fall out anyway.

They stopped for a moment at the gate of a small, fenced-in compound. There was a single guard on the gate. He looked at Belcher and then opened up. The gate was a wooden frame about ten feet tall and crisscrossed with barbed wire. The guard held an M-16, and there was a magazine in the well. After the jeeps passed through it, the guard closed and locked the gate.

Belcher shut off the engine outside a long, low hootch.

Green rubberized sandbags were stacked about halfway up the wooden walls. From the tops of the sandbags to the roof, the hootch was screened in an attempt to catch the cooling breezes. The roof was tin that had rusted and now reflected the late afternoon sun with a bright golden color. There was a screen door in the center of the front and there was a wooden boardwalk that lead to it. There was nothing on the outside of the hootch or in the compound to identify it.

As Belcher climbed out of the jeep, he said, "We use this as a staging area for the secret missions. We can keep the reporters and the riffraff out of here, although we don't get many reporters here." He smiled. "But we do get more than our share of riffraff."

Tynan got out and then reached back for his gear. "How long are we going to be here?"

Belcher shrugged. "Depends on a number of things, but from the limited information I've been given, I'll be surprised if you're here after midnight tonight." He moved toward the door, opened it, and stopped. "You'll find that new equipment has been supplied. Sterilized equipment. Leave yours here and you can pick them up on your return."

"Even the weapons? We can't leave weapons in here unattended."

"No, we'll collect those and lock them up. Now, I suggest that you take a look at what's been left here. I believe there are some written instructions too."

Tynan started to move and then stopped. "Are we going to be left here incommunicado?"

"No, sir. They'll be someone along to make sure that you have everything you need. Now, if you'll excuse me."

"Certainly." Tynan stepped through the door. It was like walking into a supply hut. There were new fatigues stacked on a table shoved against one wall. There were piles of C-rations in one corner, new shoulder harnesses and rucksacks in another, and weapons in a locked rack against the wall opposite the table. There were only a couple of chairs, a single empty table, and a ceiling fan that hung from the center of the hootch but didn't turn.

As the men entered, Tynan said, "Sterne, check the weapons. See what you think of them. Boone, look at the rucks, and Jones, see what the rations look like."

Neither Sterne nor Boone said anything, but Jones said, "Aye-aye, Skipper." Tynan moved to the table with the fatigues and found a bundle of papers that included a number of maps. He picked them up, saw that they had been created by French cartographers. He held out and asked, "Hey, Geist, can you read French?"

Geist took one of the maps, looked at it, flipped it over, and said, "No, but the symbols seem to be familiar."

"Good," said Tynan. He examined the equipment piled near him. The fatigues were of West German manufacture. There were a couple of pairs of West German binoculars, knives of Swiss design, and British field kits.

As he looked at the equipment, Tynan said, "Someone is making sure that we have everything we need, even if it isn't of American make."

He found a briefing sheet, read it quickly, and then handed it to Geist without a word. The Army sergeant read it and handed it back. Tynan said, "Let me have your attention." He watched as Sterne picked up a rifle that he didn't recognize, worked the bolt, and sighted through the scope mounted on it. Sterne then set it back in the rack and turned.

"According to the briefing package, this is a sterile mission. We'll change into the uniforms here, switch to this equipment, and leave behind everything that marks us as American servicemen.''

''Hey, Skipper,'' said Sterne, ''we've signed for these weapons. If we lose them, we're going to have to pay for them and spend weeks filling out papers.''

Tynan nodded. He wanted to tell Sterne to forget it, that everything would be worked out, but he knew how the military operated. If they assumed that somebody would take care of the problem, they would find themselves with their asses in a sling. ''We'll get receipts for the weapons. Something with the serial numbers on it and a signature saying that custody of the weapons has changed.''

''Good, Skipper,'' said Sterne.

Boone moved to the table, picked up one of the knives, and pulled it from the sheath. He tested the sharpness with the edge of his thumb and then on a sheet of paper taken from the briefing package. ''Somebody took a lot of time to put a good edge on these,'' he said.

''All the weapons are in good shape,'' added Sterne. ''They've been well cared for.''

''Uniforms look new,'' said Tynan, moving toward the table where they were stacked. ''So's the rest of the gear. The best of everything.''

''Sir,'' said Sterne, ''if I'm expected to make some long-distance shots, I'm going to have to zero the weapon. I said as much while we were in Saigon.''

Tynan looked at him and then at the racks of weapons. There were two sniper rifles. With five men, counting himself, he could have two hunter-killer teams with one man operating as a commander. A spotter and a rifle man would make up the team. Obviously all had to be done quietly, with the U.S. government prepared to deny any knowledge of who the men were if they should be caught or killed. Tynan took it a step further and figured that they wouldn't want to be captured. Killed with the bodies found, but not captured, because captured men could be made to tell who had sent them.

"I'm not sure that we'll have the opportunity to zero the weapon," said Tynan.

"Then I can't be sure that I'll hit anything. Two, three hundred yards would be no problem, but we'll want to be shooting from eight hundred to a thousand yards. If the weapon is off a fraction of an inch at that range I could miss completely. Probably would."

Tynan nodded. "Right. As soon as I can, I'll check into that."

"Who's going to use the other rifle?" asked Boone.

"I'll take it," said Geist. "I've had some experience in long-range snipering."

"Unless someone else wants to volunteer." Tynan waited and then said, "Okay, you've got it, Geist. Boone, why don't you work with Sterne, and Jones will team up with Geist. I'll act as control."

"Do you have any kind of schedule there?" asked Jones.

Tynan rifled through the papers, reading them quickly. "None."

"So we don't know how long we're going to be here or how long we'll be in the field."

"I would imagine," said Tynan, "that we'll be gone before tomorrow morning, and I would imagine that we stay out a week to ten days." He was going to say more, but turned as he heard a jeep pull up outside.

A moment later Belcher entered. "Gentlemen," he said. "Flight schedules have been moved up. You take off at dusk."

Tynan glanced at his watch and said, "That's only two, three hours."

"Before we go," interrupted Sterne, "I want a chance to zero the weapons."

"Sorry," said Belcher. "There isn't time."

"Fine," responded Sterne. "Then I'm not going."

"Of course you are," snapped Belcher. "You don't have any choice in the matter."

"Look. If I don't have the opportunity to zero the weapon, then I can't do the job, and if I can't do the job, there is no sense in going."

Belcher looked at Tynan. "Lieutenant, you had better tell your men that they will obey orders."

Tynan folded his arms and leaned back against the table. He glanced at the floor, at the dirt and mud that had been tracked into the hootch. He said, "Sterne is right. If the equipment isn't properly prepared, there is no reason to send us into the field, unless someone is intent on creating an international incident."

"Are you threatening me, Lieutenant?" asked Belcher.

"Don't be stupid. Of course not. I'm telling you that we need the opportunity to zero the weapons. Hell, the only ones that really need to be zeroed are the sniper rifles, and that should be done by the men who'll fire them. The mission demands that we take that simple step."

Now it was Belcher who looked at his watch. He pulled back the sleeve of his jungle jacket. Sweat glistened on his arm. He wiped his face with his hand. "Okay. Okay. We've got maybe thirty minutes to do it. But the plane is laid on and we can't miss that."

Tynan smiled. "Is the plane carrying any other passengers for anywhere else?"

"No. Just your team."

"Then if we're a few minutes late, they'll have to wait for us, won't they."

Belcher laughed. "Yeah, I guess they will, but if I know the Air Force boys, they won't be happy."

"Well, if it'll make them feel any better, tell them that I'm not thrilled with the way things have worked out."

Sterne and Geist took the two sniper rifles, West German-made Heckler and Kock HKPSG-1 7.62 weapons, out to the jeep. Belcher didn't want them visible to the general population of the base because there were so many American and Vietnamese civilians at Ban Me Thuot that he didn't know whom to trust. They drove out the gate, the rifles on the floor in the back of the jeep, wrapped in poncho liners.

They drove along the perimeter of the base until they came to one of the ranges. There was a bored NCO sitting in the shade of the tower, his feet propped on a wooden table. He was shirtless, his bare chest covered with a coating of perspiration. He had his fatigue cap pulled down to shade his eyes, and there was a magazine open on his lap. He didn't bother to look up as the jeep stopped near him.

Belcher got out and walked over. "We need to use your range for a few minutes."

"Range's closed," said the NCO without looking up.

"We'll only be a few minutes, we'll pick up the brass and you won't have to do a thing."

"Range's closed."

Belcher moved closer so that his shadow fell across the massive expanse of pasty white stomach. "Let me put it to you this way, Sergeant. Range's open."

Now the sergeant sat up. He closed his magazine and then pushed his cap up, out of the way. "I don't think you understood. This range is closed." He noticed that Belcher was wearing lieutenant's bars and added, "Sir."

"Sergeant, I don't have time to fuck around. I have two men who need to zero their weapons, and they will do it here. Now, if I have to call your CO, you're not going to be happy because my orders come from MACV and you'll find yourself humping the boonies with the real soldiers, not sitting back here swilling beer and making trouble."

The sergeant stood and reached for his fatigue shirt. "You're here to zero weapons?" he asked.

"Only that. Fire ten, fifteen rounds at the most."

"We should be able to accommodate that, sir," he said. "I didn't understand that. We can't get into a full-fledged practice, but zeroing a couple of weapons shouldn't be any trouble."

Now Belcher smiled. "Thank you, Sergeant. I appreciate your cooperation."

Sterne and Geist grabbed their weapons and headed to the firing line. The sergeant went to the tower and raised the bright red flag that was three feet wide and twelve feet long. That told everyone that there was firing on the range. That done, he walked slowly over to Belcher.

"We'll need targets at one hundred meters, and then we'll want to fire a couple of practice rounds at five hundred meters or so."

While the sergeant set up the targets, six of them on a man-shaped silhouette, both Sterne and Geist moved to the firing pits. Sterne dropped into one and moved the sandbars around so that he could rest his rifle on it. He removed the magazine, checked it, and then stripped all the rounds out of it. He looked it over and then put three back in.

Next to him, Geist did the same thing. He propped his rifle up, sighted through the telescope, made an adjustment to it, and then waited as the sergeant walked back from the targets.

The sergeant disappeared into the bottom of the tower and returned carrying a bright red Ping Pong paddle. He looked at the men in the firing pits, at Belcher standing well behind them, and called, "Ready on the right! Ready on the left! Ready on the firing line." He hesitated, looking right and left, and then yelled, "Commence firing."

Sterne sighted, the cross hairs of the telescope on the notch in the black box of the target. He squeezed the trigger and the weapon seemed to fire itself. He felt it recoil, slam into his shoulder. Sterne put the cross hairs in the same spot and fired again and again. The bolt locked back, signaling that the weapon was empty.

Geist fired his three shots more slowly, but he too, finished quickly.

When the sergeant saw that, he yelled, "Cease firing. Cease firing."

Sterne climbed out of his pit and walked down to the target. He examined it closely. The shot group could be covered with a quarter. That meant that the weapon fired true. It was slightly off center. Sterne made a measurement on the target and then walked back to the firing pit. He picked up the rifle and adjusted the telescopic sight by twisting the sight calibrations on the scope. That done, he dropped back into the firing pit and waited until Geist had cleared the target area before he picked up his weapon or loaded it.

When Geist was ready, the sergeant cleared the firing line again and gave them permission to fire. Sterne fired his three rounds rapidly and waited as Geist finished his. Together they walked back to the targets and checked the second group. Sterne's was in the center, but Geist's was still off slightly. They fired a third time and checked. Both weapons seemed to be set for the individual shooter. They moved the targets back to five hundred meters and took a few shots.

Sterne saw that there was no appreciable drop at five hundred meters. He knew that the ballistics of the round made it rise slightly as it left the barrel, and as the velocity was expended, the round would begin to drop. At five hundred meters, it seemed that the bullet had reached a point of equilibrium. At a thousand yards it might drop as much as a foot, though he expected it to be about half that.

He now had the information he wanted. There were a number of other calculations that should have been made—rangings at various distances from the targets, using various loads—but the sergeant was looking at them oddly, having seen the strange weapons they carried. Sterne was sure that he had all the information he needed, so he called it quits. He pulled his target up and carried it back to the tower. Then he went over to the firing pit and picked up all the brass from the expended rounds.

Finished, they walked back to the jeep. Sterne turned and saw the sergeant walking around the firing pits, as if checking for damage to his range. He didn't look up as Sterne, Geist, and Belcher climbed into the jeep.

Before he started the engine, Belcher turned toward

Sterne and asked, "You get everything you feel you need? Anything else you want to do?"

"Well, sir," said Sterne, "I would like to load my own ammo, but I guess that won't be possible. Have to make do with the factory loads."

"Is that a real problem?" asked Belcher.

"For long-range work, I would like something a little hotter than the factory loads. And you sometimes get a bad round or two, but not very often."

Belcher reached down and started the jeep. Before pulling away from the range, he turned around and saw the sergeant lowering the red banner.

It took them only a few minutes to get back to the hootch where the others waited. As they walked in the door, Tynan was standing there, dressed in the fatigues from West Germany.

"We've been alerted. As soon as you can change and get your equipment packed, we're supposed to head out to the airfield." Tynan smiled. "The balloon has gone up."

5

A covered truck pulled up outside the hootch. The driver backed up as close to the door as he could get. Then he faced to the front, ignoring everything around him. He was just the driver and that was all he was going to do. He had no desire to see the men or their equipment.

Tynan and the men who had not gone to the range had filled the rucksacks with the equipment, combat rations from West Germany, extra socks, and personal items such as toothbrushes and insect repellent. They also included the personal rifles, mainly AK-47s, that had been taken away from or surrendered by VC. They had divided up the squad equipment such as the extra ammo for the the sniper rifles and the batteries for the radio.

As Sterne and Geist entered the hootch, Tynan pointed to the fatigues that had been left on the table. "You'll have to search through those for the right size. And hurry it up."

While Sterne and Geist changed clothes, Tynan and the others began hauling their equipment and weapons out to the truck. Once they had everything loaded, Jones and Boone climbed on board. Tynan stood by the rear and waited until both Sterne and Geist appeared in the door.

"You got everything?"

Geist looked back into the hootch. "There's some uniforms left in there. Some other stuff too. You get anyone to give you a receipt for our weapons?"

"Don't worry about that," said Belcher. "I gave the lieutenant a receipt with the serial numbers of all the weapons on it. And the hootch will be cleaned out in the next couple of hours."

"Then we have everything," said Geist. He handed his sniper rifle to Sterne, climbed into the truck, and turned so he could take the rifles. Sterne handed them up and then followed them into the back.

"Drop the cover," said Belcher.

"Christ, it's hot enough in here now," said Sterne.

"It'll only be for a few minutes," said Belcher. "You won't die in there."

Sterne glanced at Tynan, who was already sweating heavily. He mopped his face with his sleeve, leaving a ragged wet stain on it. He nodded and then added, "Just do it so that we can get this over with."

Sterne dropped the cover and sat down on the wooden bench along the side of the truck. With the back cover down, the interior was dimly lit and impossibly hot. Sterne felt his head swim and was immediately bathed in sweat. He looked at the other men. They too were drenched.

They heard the engine roar to life and the truck jerked forward, stopped, and then started again. It slowed at the gate, turned, and headed for the airfield. The diesel stink from the engine seeped into the rear of the truck, choking them. Sterne leaned to the left and pushed the cover up so that they could get some air.

Moments later they stopped. Sterne stood and tossed the cover up, out of the way, and then leaned out, breathing in the fresh air. Although it was hot and muggy outside, compared with the back of the truck it was cool.

The driver came around and dropped the tailgate. Without waiting for a word from the men in the rear, he walked back to the cab.

Tynan dropped to the ground and stood staring back at the airfield. There was a C-123 with no insignia or numbers painted on it. Tynan wondered if it was the one he and the team had arrived on. The engines weren't running, but he could see the crewmen around it.

"Grab the gear and let's get it loaded."

Sterne shouldered his pack, got his weapon, and stepped close to Tynan. "I thought we were parachuting into the drop zone."

Belcher, who had followed in his jeep, overheard the comment and said, "Plans have been altered slightly. We were worried about surveillance radars picking up the aircraft during the drop—not that it would compromise you, but the plane might not make it out. There's too much in the way of antiaircraft on the border. We're sending you into Dak Pek. It's a Special Forces camp. From there you'll be flown to an LZ inside Laos by Huey helicopter."

Boone, still in the truck, shifted some of the equipment closer to the tailgate, climbed down, and then lifted out the gear. Jones and Geist followed. Once they had everything out of the truck, Belcher sent it on its way. They all stood grouped near the tower, each trying to slide into the little shade there although the sun was getting close to the horizon. They watched the Air Force crew working around the C-123 until the ramp lowered in the rear.

Belcher picked up one of the rucksacks and handed it to Tynan. "I guess you can board now." He looked into Tynan's eyes and then at each of the men with him. He held out a hand and said, "I guess I should tell you good luck. Be careful."

Tynan took his rucksack and shouldered it. "Thanks. We'll be in touch." He turned to his men. "Let's go." He glanced at Belcher and felt that there was something else that the man wanted to say. Tynan hesitated, waiting, but when Belcher didn't speak, Tynan turned. As he moved toward the aircraft, he wondered what Belcher could say. What could anyone say? Just make noise about being careful and good luck. Tynan would be careful, and luck rarely had anything to do with it.

As he neared the aircraft, one of the crewmen, wearing a flight suit, nomex gloves, and a headset, walked down the ramp, waving. Over the increasing noise of the C-123, he shouted, "This way."

Tynan looked over his shoulder. The men were following him, carrying their equipment and weapons. He stepped onto the ramp, walked toward the center of the plane, and dropped his rucksack, but held onto his weapon. The loadmaster shoved the material forward so that it rested against a pile of boxes, crates, and a couple of duffel bags. Tynan sat down, felt around for the seat belt, and buckled it. Idly he watched the rest of his men enter the aircraft and do the same thing.

Once everyone was in, the loadmaster used a

hydralic switch to raise the ramp. The crewmen swept through the aircraft, checking the belts, making sure that the equipment was tied down, and then sat down themselves. Moments later the noise from the engines increased until the sound wiped out everything else. The C-123 lurched once and then began to roll.

In minutes, they were airborne. The climb out was steep so that they were quickly out of small-arms range. They circled over the base until they were at cruising altitude and then turned to the north.

Tynan looked at his men, now cool because the aircraft was at twenty or thirty thousand feet. All seemed to be relaxed, as if they were flying to Pittsburgh. Of course, there was no reason to get scared yet. This was just another leg of a trip that had started earlier in another part of Vietnam. Tynan closed his eyes and waited for the trip to end.

Special Forces Camp A-211 at Dak Pek sat near the Laotian border. The C-123 made a steep descent onto the short dirt runway, causing the men in the back to lean forward. The aircraft touched down, bouncing once as the engine began to roar when the pilot threw them into reverse. The momentum tore at them, nearly doubling them over. And then they stopped suddenly, almost as if they had hit a brick wall. They sat motionless for a second before the pilot hit throttles and they began to taxi.

Although the plane was still moving, the loadmaster was on his feet, flipping the tie-downs out of the way, freeing the equipment that Tynan and his men had brought. When the plane stopped moving, the man shouted, "Grab it and get out. Don't move to the front, and watch the props." He hit the button for the ramp, letting it down.

Almost as Tynan and his men stepped on the ground, the ramp began to close and the aircraft began to taxi toward the end of the runway. Quickly Tynan had them move away from the runway, and as they stood there the plane roared by them, lifting upward to disappear into the clouds that were gathering overhead.

"Now what?" asked Sterne.

Tynan turned around, looking. Just off to the side was the camp. On the other side of the wire, he could see a jeep raising a cloud of red dust. It slid to a halt, the gate was opened, and the jeep raced out. As it braked, the man in the passenger's seat leaped to the ground, took a single step to catch his balance, and said, "Tynan?"

"Yeah."

"Choppers are en route." He pulled the pin on a smoke grenade but didn't toss it.

Tynan looked at the man. He was big, almost mountainous, with dark and deeply tanned skin. His jungle fatigues had faded to gray and his boots were just barely black. Tynan glanced at his face, but it told him nothing about the man. There were few wrinkles, but there were dark circles under the eyes. A hint of a mustache discolored the upper lip. He wore a green beret that was nearly plastered to the left side of his head.

"You got anything for us?" asked Tynan.

"Nope. All I know is that the choppers are inbound and you're to get on them. I don't know who you are or what you're supposed to be doing." He looked at Tynan and grinned. "Except I recognize the rifles and that gives me a clue, which is the last thing that I want."

From the distance came a quiet beat from rotor blades and the scream of turbine engines. The man threw the grenade at the end of the runway, and it began to billow a bright yellow cloud. He moved to the rear of the jeep where a radio was mounted and took the mike. ''Smoke out.''

A tinny voice, filled with static said, ''ID yellow.''

''Roger yellow.'' The man dropped the mike into the backseat of the jeep and walked over to where Tynan waited. ''When the choppers land, get on quickly. We're getting fairly close to dusk and Charlie might feel like dropping a couple of mortar rounds on us.''

''You have that problem often?''

''No. We try to keep the choppers from coming in too late in the day. Late afternoon gives Charlie all night to hide in.''

''Well, we don't want him shooting at us this early in the mission, so we'll leap on the aircraft as they touch down,'' said Tynan.

The helicopters descended toward the approach end of the runway, stopped at a hover in a swirling cloud of red dirt, debris, and yellow smoke from the grenade, and then slipped forward a couple of hundred feet. They touched down near Tynan and his men. The dust dissipated, drifting slowly to the west, and the engine roar weakened.

Overhead three gunships flew along the side of the runway and broke to the right, one covering the next in the break, as if searching for enemy gunners. Tynan could see the door gunners in the cargo compartment of the gunships, holding their M-60s pointed down and out.

Without a word, the men on the ground scooped

up their equipment and jumped into the back of the lead aircraft. As Tynan's feet touched the skids, the chopper lifted. Tynan felt hands on him, hauling him into the back of the ship. He reached out to steady himself, his hand on the ceramic seat used by the pilot as the nose dumped and the helicopter raced forward momentarily and then lifted upward.

As they reached fifteen hundred feet above the ground, Tynan got to his knees. His men were strapping on their gear, buckling the pistol belts. Tynan dragged his rucksack across the rough metal deck and worked his way into it. Once he got it seated comfortably on his shoulders, he pulled a map out of the thigh pocket of his fatigues and tapped one of the pilots on the shoulder.

The man shot a glance over his shoulder, noticed Tynan holding up his map, and leaned around the side of his seat, pulling the boom mike away from his mouth with a gloved hand. "Yeah?" he yelled over the roar of the engine and the scream of the wind.

"You know where the LZ is?"

"Yeah." The man took Tynan's map and pointed. Then he shouted, "We're going to hit three or four others. Drop in, hover through, and pop up. Confuse the hell out of Charlie. At least that's the theory."

Tynan nodded in exaggerated motions. "I understand."

"You probably will jump off in the second or third. Crew chief will tell you."

Again Tynan nodded.

The pilot looked out the window and then back. "We're going to drop down now, low level. We're coming up on the border." The man grinned as the bottom seemed to drop out and the helicopter fell out of the sky.

Through the windshield, Tynan watched the ground come up rapidly. Then the chopper leveled, dodging the tall trees, the skids seemingly only inches above the canopy of the jungle. They swerved to the right, the helicopter rolling up on the side so that Tynan could look down, out the cargo compartment door. He could feel gravity forcing him down for a moment and then he seemed to be weightless as they topped a tall tree and dropped again. He slipped back, toward the troop seat, so that he could grab one of the supports for it and hold on.

They was a whoop to the right and he saw Sterne sitting there, staring out the cargo compartment at the growing dusk, a hand on his helmet as if the wind rushing through could rip it from his head. Sterne was leaning forward, one hand clinging onto the edge of the troop seat. His eyes squinted because of the wind, but he was obviously enjoying himself.

The crew chief leaned around the transmission wall from his well on the side of the ship and shouted, "We've just crossed the border. We're in Laos."

Tynan looked at him and nodded, but didn't say anything. He was suddenly sick to his stomach. He wanted to throw up, and he clamped his teeth together. He leaned to the right so that the fresh breeze blowing in the open cargo compartment doors could slap him in the face. He closed his eyes, not wanting to see, but his stomach seemed to turn over and he opened them again. He stared upward, at the blackening sky. He could see a couple of the brighter stars overhead.

He attempted a glance down, and out to the left, far out, he could see the twinkling of a green running light on the side of one of the gunships. For an instant, Tynan thought the pilot was incredibly stupid. Turning on the nav lights while violating enemy airspace. Suddenly he realized that they had to turn them on. They had to be able to see the other ships in the formation. What a way to make a living.

He smiled then, realizing that all that had taken his mind, even momentarily, off his stomach. But then he noticed that they weren't as low as they had been. It was darker now, almost completely black, and the pilots had climbed upward to avoid smashing into some unseen terrain feature.

Suddenly they broke to the right in a tight turn that smashed him down, against the deck. He could see a stream of bright green tracers arcing upward, flashing in the night. A second stream joined the first, criss-crossing with it. Tynan thought that they were far out, nowhere near the aircraft, but wasn't sure. Tracers were deceptive at night.

More green and white tracers appeared in front of them, and as the helicopter dodged to the left, the lights on one of the gunships disappeared. Seconds later there were flashes near the front as rockets fired. Tynan tried to see where they hit, but they were lost in the blackness of the jungle below them, masked by the thick canopy.

Again they seemed to drop. The blackness of the ground seemed to merge with the deep, dark grays of the sky. They slowed, inches from the ground, hovering, and then shot upward until they were clear. The jungle below twinkled and sparkled like the night sky as the enemy fired machine guns and AKs at the sound of the helicopter's engines. Tracers lanced upward, tumbling out of sight.

There was a roar to the left that sounded like a buzzsaw gone berserk. Tynan saw a tongue of flame at the side of one of the gunships as it fired its minigun. The ruby tracers, spaced every fourth round, looked like the red ray from a science fiction weapon. It danced down, covering the ground in short bursts like raindrops. It was an impressive sight.

For the third time they fell out of the sky. The crew chief reached around and tapped Tynan's shoulder. "This one is it," he called.

Tynan nodded and checked the safety on his weapon. He jacked a round into the chamber, buckled the strap on his helmet so that he wouldn't lose it when he leaped from the chopper, and waited. He had forgotten about his stomach during the show put on by the gunships and Charlie.

A second later, the helicopter came to a hover. Tynan leaped, misjudged the distance to the ground, and landed hard. He rolled and came up on one knee as the helicopter dropped its nose. There was a blast of rotorwash and a roar of turbine that quickly disappeared. Tynan saw a flash of light, saw a couple of tracers shoot skyward. Then it was quiet. No noise at all. No sound from the aircraft, from animals or insects. A chilling quiet that made him think that he had lost his hearing.

He stood up and glanced behind him. In the dark, he could see the shapes of two of his men. Without speaking to them, he began to work his way off the LZ, listening for something that would tell him that there was trouble around. Listening for the snap of a twig, a muffled voice, the metallic click of a bolt. But there were no sounds.

At the edge of the jungle, he stopped and dropped to one knee. Behind him, he could see his men. They fanned out, their weapons ready. Tynan got up and moved forward. He stopped again, waiting, but there was nothing there. In seconds the whole patrol was in the jungle, off the LZ.

Tynan moved close to Sterne, put his lips next to the man's ear, and said, ''We'll camp here for the night. Check the LZ at first light to make sure that we left nothing on it.''

6

They moved only fifty or sixty meters off the LZ, using the jungle that surrounded it for protection. Without speaking, they took up positions, pairing off so that one man could sleep while the other watched. Tynan teamed up with Sterne and Boone and they shared one watch in three.

They passed the night quietly, listening to the growing sounds in the jungle around them as the animals and insects filtered back in. Tynan took his turn at guard, lying on his stomach under the broad leaves of a huge bush, staring into the inky blackness of the jungle. Overhead was nothing but the inter-woven leaves of the canopy that let in no light from the stars or the moon. Tynan was relieved by Sterne and then went to sleep. Near dawn he was awakened by the changing sounds in the jungle as the monkeys and birds hidden in the treetops slowly came awake. He lay on his back, staring up, but could see nothing of the sky through the triple canopy. He realized slowly that it was getting lighter around him.

Tynan sat up and soon saw that Boone was sitting

near him, eating breakfast from a C-ration can, using the white plastic spoon supplied with it. Hollywood liked the image of the soldier using his combat knife to eat the meal, but that only dulled the blade and cut the mouth. Tynan glanced to the right and saw Jones leaning against the thick trunk of a teak tree, an OD can in his hand, eating peaches. The others were lost in the mists of the jungle. Tynan quietly opened his rucksack, found a can of scrambled eggs. He dumped a couple of packets of salt on them, figuring that it would make them edible and that the extra salt in the humidity of the jungle wouldn't hurt him.

With breakfast finished, Tynan eased out of hiding and worked his way back to the LZ. He crouched in the jungle and then stretched out on the ground. He worked his way forward until he could look out and see the short grass and small bushes. He let his eyes wander slowly from one end to the other. There seemed to be evidence that a helicopter had landed. A squashed bush, crushed by one of the skids, was near the center of the LZ, and Tynan thought about using his knife to remove it. But he didn't like the idea of exposing himself on the open ground. A broken bush didn't mean that much. If Charlie found it quickly enough, he might be able to guess about how long ago the bush had been smashed, but Tynan didn't see how that would help him.

To be on the safe side, he checked everything a final time. There were no pieces of equipment lying in the open. Tynan withdrew slowly, working his way back to the rest of the men. Around him, he heard nothing other than the normal jungle sounds. He saw nothing. They had slipped in and no one seemed to know that they were there.

As he approached his campsite, he wondered if the

helicopters had gotten out safely. Once Tynan and his men were out and the choppers had disappeared, there was no way for him to know. If they had been shot down on one of the other diversionary landings, Tynan wouldn't have seen or heard it. As he thought of that, he wondered if the pilots had written the landing locations on their maps. He wondered exactly how much information was written on those maps and how valuable they would be to the VC if they captured them. He wished he had thought of it earlier so that he could have asked.

But then he decided that it didn't matter because he had no reason to suspect that the helicopters had been shot down, that the maps had been captured, or that there was anything on them that would compromise the mission.

Tynan entered the tiny perimeter. He could see Jones near his tree, but the rest of the men seemed to have vanished. Tynan wanted to shout at them, tell them that it was time to get going, but he didn't want to speak out loud. He snapped his fingers once, the sound seeming overly loud in the jungle.

There was a rustling of leaves, and Boone appeared. Tynan pointed to the southwest, toward the area where Geist had seen the NVA buildup. Tynan pulled out his map, checked, and then waved his hand, telling Boone to move.

As Boone began to disappear into the jungle, Sterne fell in behind him, six or seven meters separating them. Geist joined up and then Jones. Tynan waited until Jones had nearly vanished and fell in with them.

The pace was slow, each man being careful not to make a sound. With the triple canopy jungle over them, the sun was not a factor. The jungle steamed with the saunalike heat, but the sun wasn't baking them. The pace, restricted by the density of the jungle, made the walking easier. Tynan would tap his forehead with his sleeve, drying the sweat, but after an hour, his shirt was soaked.

Boone stopped to rest. Tynan moved up to find out if there was a problem, but Boone shook his head. Tynan crouched down, near the trunk of a palm, wiped his face on the inside of his sleeve near his elbow, and then opened one of his canteens. The water was warm and tasted like plastic. Tynan wasn't sure that the military move from metal to plastic was such a good idea, although he had to admit that the plastic didn't make as much noise as the metal canteens, and the dark color didn't reflect the light.

After ten minutes, Boone got to his feet and began moving through the jungle again. The pace was slow as he pushed the branches of bushes out of the way rather than hacking through them. It kept their progress slow, but it also would prevent the enemy from finding their trail easily.

It was midmorning when they stepped on it. There was a sudden explosion in the front. Tynan dived to the side, rolled, and came up facing the direction of the explosion as shooting broke out around him. As the bullets started ripping through the trees around him, he could see a small cloud of black smoke and red dust drifting upward. He couldn't see any of his men though. The jungle concealed them.

Tynan crawled to the south carefully, keeping low, his eyes flipping right and left. He could see nothing of the enemy. The firing from the AKs and SKS's had tapered slightly. He was waiting for answering fire from his men, but heard nothing. He stopped when he saw a body lying on the ground in front of him. He couldn't tell who it was, but he could see a ragged stain of bright red on the back and side.

From somewhere a voice shouted a command in Vietnamese and the shooting stopped for a moment. There was a groan and a single rifle shot. Tynan eased back, deeper into the jungle. He could see nothing and hear nothing. It was as if time had suddenly stopped. It was as if he was suddenly blinded.

For a moment, Tynan collapsed face down on the soft, wet dirt of the jungle floor, letting the musty odor, like a freshly dug grave, wash over him. He slipped the safety off his rifle and then quietly unsnapped the flap over his combat knife. Slowly, he rolled to his left and slipped the sling of his rifle over his shoulder. Then he rose to his hands and knees to survey the area.

He could hear movement in the jungle now and the low whisper of voices speaking Vietnamese. Tynan worked his way to the trunk of a tree that was surrounded by clinging vines and got to his feet, his back to the tree. Turning his head slowly, using his eyes rapidly, he saw one of the Vietnamese coming toward him, a short, stocky man wearing the dark green of the NVA, carrying a new-looking AK-47, the folding bayonet extended.

The man poked the rifle into a bush, stirred it around as if looking for someone, and then moved on. He cautiously approached the tree where Tynan hid, searching for the survivors of the ambush.

When he was close, his back to the tree, Tynan stepped out and grabbed him from behind, lifting the enemy's chin, his fingers over the man's mouth and pinching his nose shut. With a single fluid stoke, Tynan cut the man's throat from left to right, the blade biting deep. As the man fell back against Tynan's chest, the blood gushing down over his shirt, Tynan drove the blade up, under the man's ribs above the kidney, piercing the heart.

Slowly, he lowered the enemy's body to the jungle floor, rolling it to its side under one of the broad-leaf bushes. He took the man's weapon, was going to eject the round in the chamber and throw it away, but thought better of it. It was just that much more spare ammo for him. He slung the weapon as he glanced at the body. He looked at the man's face for the first time and was shocked by the waxy look of the skin. There was the hint of a mustache along the upper lip and whiskers sprouting on the chin. Tynan had felt none of it when he put his hand over the man's mouth to keep him from crying out.

As he turned, he saw another man rushing at him, head down, bayonet extended. Tynan spun to meet the threat, used his forearm to push the barrel of the AK away from him. As the VC tried to stop, Tynan slashed at the throat with his knife. There was a spurt of bright red blood that splashed him. The man fell to one knee, dropping his weapon. Both hands were on the side of his neck, trying to stop the bleeding. Tynan kicked him in the side and as the enemy toppled, Tynan finished him with the knife, jamming into the man's chest.

He dodged to the right, back toward the path where he had seen the body of one of his men. He crouched at the side of a tree, and through gaps in the foliage, he could see three of the enemy kneeling by the body. Tynan slipped the AK from his shoulder, quietly checked the safety and bolt and then aimed. He squeezed off a short burst, catching the enemy chest high. The first two toppled back, into the vegetation. The third was on his feet. Three rounds stitched their way across his stomach, blowing out his back. As he dropped, blood blossomed on his shirt. He fell next to the dead American.

As he finished shooting, Tynan dived for cover, crawling rapidly to the south. He heard a shout in Vietnamese and a single shot that didn't come from either an AK or SKS. It meant that at least one of his men still survived.

A shout erupted from somewhere. Tynan pulled one of his grenades and waited. There was a grunt and a muffled command in Vietnamese. Tynan yanked the pin and threw the grenade at the sound of the voice. He flattened himself and counted silently. He was aware of the heat of the jungle, of the sweat on his face and under his arms, of the lack of normal jungle noise. He thought that the grenade should have detonated and wanted to look up, but forced himself to stay down. He was convinced that the grenade was a dud.

And then there was an explosion. Debris rained through the jungle, showering the area as it hit the leaves of the bushes. A shriek followed, and then a wild burst of firing. Tynan heard the bullets passing harmlessly over his head, smacking into the trees. There was an answering shot, a single burst from an AK, and two more rifle shots.

Tynan moved to the path and could see the body of one of his men, the three Vietnamese lying near it. Noticing the hand of a fourth man, he eased forward then and saw a second American lying face down. It looked like Boone, but Tynan wasn't sure. He could see no blood on the uniform, could see no wounds at all, but there was a stillness about the body that suggested it was dead.

Through the trees, he saw a flicker of movement

and a flash of black pajamas. He rolled to his right side and fired a burst into the jungle. A second later he heard a crash that sounded like a body falling into the vegetation.

Tynan got to his hands and knees, listened, but heard no one moving. He let his eyes search the jungle around him and saw nothing. Finally he got to his feet and leaped forward, his foot nearly touching one of the bodies before he dived into the jungle on that side of the ambush. He rolled once and flattened himself on the ground waiting for the shooting to begin, but no one shot at him. He looked at the bodies. The one surrounded by the dead VC and NVA was Sterne. There was no doubt of that. He could see the face. A blood-covered face with a neat black hole in the forehead.

Having established the identity of one of the dead, Tynan moved forward, trying to see the second body. He heard a movement near him. A quiet rustling of the leaves. Tynan stopped, looked to the right. He could see a pair of sandals. For a moment, Tynan thought about taking the man with his knife, silently, but decided that he wanted to know more about the enemy force. He had no idea how large the ambush party was, where they were, or where his own men were. If any of them still survived.

Again he rolled to his side. He flipped the selector on the AK to single shot and aimed at the man's ankle. As he pulled the trigger, he saw blood explode on the dirty skin. A moment later the man fell, both hands around his wounded foot. He looked toward Tynan and his eyes widened as he saw the American. There was a moment when it seemed that he was going to shout. Tynan put a second round into the man's face, smashing his nose and breaking a couple of his teeth. The VC flopped to his back as his blood spurted once.

Tynan waited, but there was no return fire and no other movement. Slowly he got to his feet and retreated from the trail, getting deeper into the jungle. He leaned his back against a palm tree and let his eyes roam, searching for the enemy. Waiting for a chance to counterambush them. He could see a slowly drifting cloud of blue smoke from the shooting, rising upward. He could easily see Sterne's body, but not that of the other American. He heard nothing around him.

Time seemed to stand still. Tynan realized that he was thirsty. He wanted a drink of water. He didn't care if it was warm and tasted like plastic. He just needed it, but now that he seemed to be safe, he didn't want to move. He stared at the boot on Sterne's foot and then shifted his gaze to the bodies of the VC around him. He listened carefully but heard no one else in the jungle. The mission was over, he realized. There was no way he could carry on with two of his men dead. Two that he knew about. The rest could be dead too.

Slowly sound returned. A quiet buzzing at first. One or two flies slipping through the heavy, wet, jungle air. But these were joined by more and more until it seemed that there were a hundred thousand flies searching for a place to land. Searching for the dead.

Tynan slipped to the ground so that he was sitting. There was a rustling to his left and he turned to face it, his rifle held up and ready. He waited patiently, thinking about his grenades and his water and the dead men in front of him. There was a single flash of movement, but Tynan didn't shoot at it because he still didn't know who was where.

A second later Geist appeared. He had lost his helmet and blood and dirt were smeared on his face. Sweat had soaked his uniform. He swung his rifle at Tynan and then recognition dawned on his face. He grinned.

Tynan got to his feet and when Geist was close, he whispered, "We've got two dead."

Geist nodded his understanding and replied, "Jones is wounded. Round through and through. I've got him patched, but he's not going to do us any good."

"Where was he hit?"

"Shoulder. Tore it up pretty good. I'm not sure he'll ever have full use again."

"Enemy?" He pulled at the snaps on one of his canteens, took it out, and drank deeply. The water was warm and tasted like plastic, just as he knew it would, but somehow it was quite refreshing.

Geist shrugged. "Bodies around but haven't seen a thing. I think they split."

"Or we got them all."

"There is that," said Geist. "Now what?"

Tynan looked at Sterne's body. "I guess that ends it. No way we can complete the mission with over half the team either dead or wounded."

"And?"

"We escape and evade out of here."

"There was a lot of shooting around here. Maybe we should get out now."

"We can't leave the bodies," said Tynan. "We've got to either carry them out or bury them."

"Yes, sir," said Geist. "Don't leave the dead in the field. Waste the living to save the dead."

"Sergeant," said Tynan, "on a covert operation it

is not a good idea to leave clues scattered around if you can police them up.''

"Sorry, sir. What do we do?"

"Carry the bodies a couple of hundred meters away from here and bury them."

Geist nodded. "I'm not sure if Jones is going to be able to walk. He lost a lot of blood."

"We'd better do something," said Tynan. He moved toward the path. He looked at Sterne again and then back at Boone. He began to roll him over but then stopped. Shrapnel and bullets had ripped open Boone's chest and stomach. There was no way to pick up the body without it falling to pieces.

"We could blow them up," said Geist quietly.

Tynan looked up at him but didn't speak. To blow them apart seemed to be doing the VC's job for them. Mutilate the dead. Then Tynan realized that his plan was no less barbaric. Drop them into unmarked graves. Blowing them up kept them out of the hands of the enemy, and that was the only thing that Tynan was worried about. That somehow, if the VC and NVA recovered the bodies, they could use them for propoganda.

Then he realized that there wasn't much he could do to blow them up. They had no explosives other than hand grenades and anything that they might find on the bodies of the enemy. The only thing he could do was mutilate them so badly that the enemy wouldn't be able to exploit them. It was all he could do for them.

He moved to Sterne's body and pulled it back to lay it next to Boone. He then checked a few of the dead VC and NVA, taking their weapons, searching their packs for extra grenades, finding a few. As he was trying to work out a way to use the most grenades without endangering himself or Geist, he realized that he was being stupid. Sterne and Boone could be used for a final ambush. Booby-trap them and take a few of the enemy out. Tynan grinned at that. He knew Sterne would approve. Sterne could continue to kill even though he was dead himself. And the resulting explosions would mutilate the bodies so they would be of no value to the enemy.

Quickly he rigged the bodies. He pulled the pins of the grenades and slipped them into position under the dead. As Charlie tried to move them, the safety spoons would fly, arming the grenades. Seconds later they would explode. He wished that he had a couple of smoke grenades so that he could use their fuses. The instant the safety spoon was released, the grenade went off. Smoke grenades just billowed smoke, but a regular grenade would detonate immediately with a smoke grenade fuse.

When Tynan finished, he helped Geist sweep the field, checking the rest of the enemy dead, taking their weapons and extra ammo. The last thing Tynan wanted to do was carry several AK-47s through the jungle, but then he didn't want to leave them for the enemy to retrieve. If they came to a deep pond or river, he could drop them in and deny them to the enemy.

They found twelve dead VC and two NVA. One of the NVA soliders was an officer. Tynan pulled the collar tabs from his uniform, stole his pistol and his watch that seemed to contain some kind of military crest or insignia. He thought that it might be of use to the boys in intelligence, if he lived long enough to give it to them.

Geist took him into the jungle, where they found Jones sitting against a tree, his face pale and covered with sweat. He looked up as they approached and tried to smile. The right side of his uniform was bloodstained and ripped, revealing his shoulder. There was a pressure bandage tied there in an amateurish looking fashion, but it seemed to be effective. The blood had stopped flowing.

"How you doing?" asked Tynan.

"Okay, Skipper. How are the others?" He didn't look up. He seemed to be weak, but was struggling not to show it.

"I'm afraid they didn't make it," said Tynan quietly. "We have to leave them here, but I've booby-trapped them. I think they would approve of the tactic. You feel up to a little traveling?"

"I think so. What about the mission?"

"I would think that the mission has been compromised. I don't see how we can complete it. I hope they put some other teams into the area as backup."

"We're going home?" asked Geist. "Just quit and pull out? Just like that?"

"Not quite that simple," said Tynan. "I was given the names of a couple villages where we can get aid. I think the move of the hour is to head for the closest. Once there we'll try to make contact with our control and tell them we're down and hope that there is a backup around."

Geist shot Tynan a glance. "You never mentioned anything about friendly villages in the area."

"No. We're not supposed to use them unless it's an emergency and this seems to be one."

Jones struggled to stand up, swayed once as Geist leaped toward him to steady him. Jones grinned and said, "Thanks. Stood up too fast."

Tynan glanced at his watch, peeling back the camouflage covering on it. He was surprised to see that the ambush and fighting had taken less than an hour. It wasn't quite noon, but Tynan wasn't hungry. He got out his map and studied it. The detail in Laos wasn't as fine as it could be. But the village was marked, and Tynan could see that they were fifteen or twenty klicks to the northeast of it. They could be there by dusk if they pushed it as hard as they could. The problem was Jones. Tynan didn't know how much strength the young man would have. That could slow them down, especially if they had to carry him all the way.

There seemed to be other things that should be done, but Tynan couldn't think of what they should be. They had already stayed longer than they should have. The firing would alert any enemy in the area. They had to get out, even if it was only to move a klick or two.

"Compass heading of one nine five," said Tynan. "Tom, you begin to feel weak, you sing out. I don't want you to collapse on us. We get to that village and we should be able to find some medical aid."

"Aye-aye, sir," said Jones.

"Then let's do it."

7

It was nearly midnight when they halted for the last time. They had stopped in the middle of the afternoon to let Jones rest, and while he slept, Tynan and Geist made a stretcher out of two saplings and a poncho liner. They carried Jones through the rest of the afternoon, stopping only long enough for Geist and Tynan to rest and drink their water. They skipped eating their evening meal because they figured they could eat all they wanted once they reached the friendly camp.

The travel had been miserable. They had wanted to stay away from trails and paths, and while Jones was able to walk, they were able to avoid them. The jungle in places was a hopeless tangle of interwoven bushes, plants, vines, and trees that became an almost impenetrable wall. They detoured around the thicket, but had to cut their way through some of it, setting the stretcher down to use their machetes, and were forced to game trails in the rest. Progress was slow, hot work.

Tynan found himself nearly gasping for breath, his

mouth filled with cotton. He felt light-headed and sick to his stomach. His arms ached, and he was covered with sweat, making him more miserable. All he wanted to do was drop to the ground to rest, to find a place where it was cool. He forced himself onward, wondering how Jones managed to stay on his feet—since he had demanded that he be allowed to walk.

Moments later, Jones collapsed, lying face down on the jungle floor. He was conscious, but his face was pale and he wasn't sweating.

Geist moved close, looked at Jones, and then quietly suggested that they carry him the rest of the way no matter what he said. He was in no shape to walk. Tynan nodded his approval.

They had a hard time convincing Jones to use the stretcher. Tynan finally convinced him by making it an order. From that point, they made good progress but were forced from an overland route to the various game trails and paths. Each time they came to one, they examined it, searching for clues that someone had used it recently.

Now, according to the map, they were within a couple of hundred yards of the village. Geist was facing the way they had come, watching for signs that they had been followed. Jones slept on his stretcher and Tynan crouched among the bushes and trees, trying to see some indication that there was a village somewhere nearby. A light, some noise, a fire—anything.

After studying the black jungle for a couple of minutes, Tynan slipped back to the stretcher. He put his face only inches from Jones, trying to see him. He could hear Jones breathing. It sounded deep and rhythmic, as if Jones was asleep. There were no indications that Jones was in any immediate danger from his wound. They would have to treat it properly soon, find some medicine for him and some real medical help, but a couple more hours, one way or the other, shouldn't make a difference.

Tynan moved forward again, feeling his way along. He worked his way toward where the village should have been. The map, the terrain, everything, indicated that the village should be a couple of hundred yards—at the very most—in front of them, but still there was no sign.

Carefully, Tynan took his binoculars from their case. They were supposed to gather the available light, enhance it, and make the surroundings brighter, easier to see. Except he was in triple canopy jungle and there didn't seem to be any light available. No moon, no stars, no lights from the inhabitants.

If this was the right location, and it was a militarized village, there would be guards out, men scattered through the trees in listening posts to prevent the VC and NVA from sneaking up on them to wipe them out. If it was just a friendly village, people who would help Americans because they were Americans, then there might not be any sentries. Tynan and his men could just walk in.

He peeled back the camouflage band on his watch and looked at the glowing numbers of the dial. It would be light in only a couple of hours, Jones seemed to be resting comfortably, no longer bothered by the heat and humidity of the steambath jungle. But even with the sun gone, Tynan was still miserable. He decided that if he ever got out of Laos, he would take an assignment in Canada or Norway or Alaska. Anywhere they had winter and snow and no blast-furnace weather.

Geist loomed out of the dark and crouched near Tynan. He put his lips against Tynan's ear and said, "What now?"

"Wait for morning and then walk in."

"You get any kind of recognition signals or code words for these guys?"

Tynan shook his head but realized that Geist would never be able to see it. "No. I believe the thinking was that we wouldn't need them because we wouldn't be coming here. Besides, this is only one of five villages they told me about. I don't think they have much luck coordinating code words with the locals. At least that's what I was told."

"So how do we approach them?"

"When it's light, we just walk in. Let them see us coming and look as innocent as we can."

"Fucking great plan," said Geist.

"You got a better one, I'd like to hear it."

"Don't get me wrong. I understand that it's the best we can do. I just love these missions where we're given half the shit we're supposed to have. No code words. Equipment from a bunch of foreign governments like that's going to fool anyone, and now half the team dead."

There were a dozen things that Tynan wanted to say to Geist. He was tired of the complaining. He was tired of listening to him second-guessing everyone. He was tired of the man talking in the jungle when they should be quiet, listening for the enemy. He turned to look at Geist, a dark shape in a black background. He didn't speak. He realized that Geist hadn't been complaining all that much and that he was right. It was a great fucking mission when they gave him half the information he needed.

A moment later Geist slid off, heading back to his

rearguard position. Tynan heard him only when he was right next to him. Otherwise Geist moved like a ghost, gliding through the thickest jungle like some kind of ethereal mist.

Tynan went back to watching the jungle. He could hear the quiet noise of insects moving, their tiny claws scraping on the thick leaves of the jungle vegetation. There were other sounds, animals moving around, some searching for plants, others searching for those that ate the plants. Tynan let his forehead rest momentarily on his forearm, his nose only inches from the damp soil of the jungle floor. He knew that he was taking a chance because he hadn't slept in so long, but he just needed to relax his neck muscles and close his eyes. Just for a second. Just a little rest.

He sprang awake, his muscles singing, his heart pounding, and his breathing rapid and shallow. He listened closely, but heard nothing near him. He knew what had happened. He had dozed off and a moment later his brain had demanded he awaken. He had seen men on ship do that. They would be lying quietly on their bunks and then seem to explode upward, snapping themselves off their bunks. The other sailors would disintegrate into laughter, calling the phenomenon the screaming meemies.

The dawn came slowly, the sunlight filtering through the vegetation of the jungle. Tynan realized that he could see shapes around him that slowly became trees. He looked at his watch, saw that it was nearly sunup, and worked his way back to the stretcher. Jones slept on as if he didn't have a worry in the world.

Geist appeared and asked, "Is it time?"

"Yeah," said Tynan. "I think it's time."

Together they moved to the southeast, separating

slightly. They halted, watched and moved again. Tynan was searching for anything that would show him the position of the village or the guard outposts. When he had gone a hundred meters, he decided that he wasn't going to find it easily. He heard nothing other than the normal sounds of the jungle coming awake, although there wasn't the riot of noise that he had heard in the past in other parts of Southeast Asia.

He retreated to the stretcher and waited for Geist. As he approached, he nodded and then said, ''I think I've got them spotted.''

They lifted the stretcher. Jones opened his eyes, moved his hand, and groaned in pain. He looked pale and still wasn't sweating. He didn't look as if he was resting comfortably, but he was resting. Tynan was worried about him, but didn't say anything. Jones started to lift his head to look at his surroundings, but let it drop back and seconds later seemed to be asleep again.

With Geist leading, they dodged around the worst of the jungle vegetation. It took them forty minutes to travel forty meters. Then Geist gestured, indicating that he wanted to set the stretcher on the ground.

As Tynan stepped closer to him, he pointed and said, ''Through there. Follow me.''

Geist pushed past a large bush, dropped to the ground, and crawled forward. Tynan followed him. A moment later he could see a thin line of pale blue smoke rise through the jungle, hit the canopy, and dissipate.

He worked his way forward, stopped at the base of a palm and saw the tops of a line of hootches. He looked at Geist, shrugged, and moved closer. There was a low wall around the village, a fence of woven branches that appeared to be flimsy. It might slow down an assault but it certainly wouldn't stop it. Then he remembered something that he read somewhere. A man in a battle would feel safer if he could hide behind something. It made no difference that it was flimsy and would be penetrated by bullets. Give him a little protection, no matter how imagined it might be, and he would be braver.

Geist slipped into position next to him and asked, "This the place?"

"Has to be," said Tynan.

"So how we going to do this?"

"Why don't you wait here? I'll approach and you can see what kind of reception I get. If they're friendly, I'll bring them out and we'll collect you and Jones."

"And if they're not?"

"Then it's up to you to get Jones out of here. You'll have to E and E back to South Vietnam. You can see that someone notifies Walker that I was killed."

"And I get to E and E a good thirty, forty klicks," said Geist.

Tynan grinned at him. "No one said it was going to be easy when you volunteered for the job."

Geist shook his head slowly. "Somehow I don't remember volunteering for shit."

"Yeah, well there you are. Why don't you drop back where you can watch me, but if they turn out to be bad guys, they won't have a fix on your position. I'll give you about five minutes."

"Yes, sir," said Geist. "Good luck."

Tynan didn't respond. He glanced at his watch and nodded. He didn't watch Geist move off because he didn't want to know where he was going. He just watched the second hand sweep around the dial of his watch and wished for the hundredth time that it were cooler in the jungle. He wondered why all his assignments dropped him into the jungle. The jungles of Africa or the jungles of Southeast Asia. Lousy environments that had a hundred new dangers, from poisonous snakes and insects to carnivorous animals to all kinds of diseases that could kill or injure.

When Geist had his five minutes, Tynan got to his feet, brushed the dirt and mud from the front of his uniform, checked the safety on his weapon and slung it. He stepped forward, angled toward a place where the undergrowth thinned. There was a sudden flapping near him and he dropped to one knee, grabbing for his weapon as a bird broke cover. He grinned at it, wanted to laugh out loud as the adrenaline coursed through him, making him nervous. Making him want to run.

Tynan stood up and began edging his way toward the fence. Still he saw no humans. Smoke indicating fire. But no voices. No movement.

He moved closer, looking for a gate. The jungle thinned until it was no worse than a light forest. He could see that the ground around the village had been cleared and that pungi stakes, angling away from the fence, had been planted by the thousands around the perimeter. He spotted loopholes in the fence for firing positions, and he noticed that the fence was not straight but bowed inward so that the men on the corners could catch attackers in the center in a crossfire. This wasn't the haphazard arrangement typical of the untrained, but a well-thought-out, well-executed defensive plan.

There was a narrow path through the pungi field. It was not a straight trail, but one that swept back and forth so that attackers couldn't use it as an avenue for the assault. Tynan stopped at the beginning of it, watching the village. Everything about it suggested a military operation, which meant there should have been guards, but he could see none.

He left the protection of the trees and stepped on the path. He walked along it slowly, his eyes shifting along the wall, looking for signs of the villagers. When he was fifty feet from the gate that was so well constructed that it masqueraded as part of the fence, there was a shout.

Tynan halted and lifted his hands. He waited but there was nothing more from the village. He could see nothing along the fence and heard nothing behind it. He wondered what was happening back there and wondered if he should continue moving toward the village without some idea of what was going on.

A minute later, the gate slid open, revealing part of the interior. Tynan could see a single building, a long, low structure that was raised two or three feet off the ground by a series of wooden stilts. There was one man visible near the building, but he quickly disappeared.

As Tynan took a step forward, a man appeared in the gate. He was a tall man with a long, tangled beard and long, shaggy hair. He was wearing a loin-cloth and rubber sandals made from old truck tires. When another of the villagers fell in next to him, Tynan realized that the first man was a good foot taller than the second and his skin was a good deal lighter.

Still he hadn't seen a weapon. Tynan began to ease forward, walking slowly and carefully, giving the men in the village a chance to halt him if they wanted to, but no one spoke until he was only ten feet away.

"Who are you?" asked the tall man in perfect English.

Tynan wasn't sure what he should say. It was a covert mission into Laos with sterile equipment. Uniforms and weapons from European manufacturers. And there were orders to maintain that secrecy at all cost.

"Mark Tynan," he said. "United States Navy."

"You a downed flyer?" asked the man.

"No. Not really."

"Come on in," said the man, stepping back so that he was concealed behind the fence.

Tynan was tempted to turn, to look into the jungle, but that would only tell the villagers that there was someone else out there. Tynan walked to the gate, halted just outside of it. He looked through, seeing a series of hootches up on stilts, notched logs leading into the entrances. Near the center of the village was a single large fire giving off the smoke, and surrounding it were several bare-breasted women with bright-colored cloths wrapped around their waists. He could see a couple of armed men. They were holding old bolt action rifles with an ease that suggested they knew how to use them.

"Come on in, Mark Tynan of the United States Navy," said the man who had spoken.

The way the man said it scared Tynan. He wondered if he should have left off the Navy part. The man seemed to be a Caucasian and spoke with an American accent. The last thing he expected was a Russian, but he supposed that it could be possible. That was, until the man said, "I won't bite. I'm on your side."

Tynan stepped through the gate. To his left were three men with rifles pointing at him. These were not old bolt action weapons but newer, automatic rifles undoubtedly supplied by the U.S. government. To the right was another one standing next to the tall man.

"Who are you?" asked Tynan.

"Name's not important," said the man. "What can I do for you?"

"I'm afraid that I've gotten myself separated from my unit and need some assistance getting back to it."

"Uh-huh. You're out there running around the jungle by yourself? Running around the jungle in Laos all by yourself because you got lost?"

"Yes." Tynan looked at the man. His speech pattern was a little strange. Like his mouth was stiff from not speaking English for a long time. His English was perfect; he just spoke it slowly, as if it was a second language for him.

The man turned to the villager next to him and rattled off a long string of singsong sentences. The villager slung his weapon and then moved to close the gate.

"Who are you?" asked Tynan again.

"Let's just say that I'm on your side. I've received a radio transmission that suggested you'd be by." The man glanced at the natives and then asked, "Where are the others?"

As he got close to the man, he noticed blue eyes. But then Russians could have blue eyes, and as he thought that, he shook himself. The man seemed to know a lot, asking for the others. Tynan knew that the CIA had men stationed with some of the villagers in Laos, training anticommunist guerrillas to fight the NVA and the Pathet Lao. Most of them were Special Forces officers on special assignments. He had been told that much by Smith in Cholon.

"We have two dead and one wounded. I've got the wounded man with me. What are the chances of getting some medical attention for him?"

The man looked at the gate, as if waiting for the others to appear. "Only medical help is me. I've had some basic first aid and a couple of courses given to medics in the Army, but that's about it. I have some medicines."

"Can we get him evacked?"

"That might be a problem. We've got a makeshift airfield, but we don't like to use it. Gives the enemy too many clues about us, but that's a possibility. I'll send a couple of my men out with you." Again he fired some of the singsong language. Two of the men slung their rifles and moved to the gate. "They'll help you get your party inside."

An hour later Tynan sat on the rough wood floor of one of the long buildings, sitting across from the man who still refused to give a name. Geist sat next to him, eating rice from the center of a broad, green leaf. Four women, the youngest and cleanest, stood behind them, holding pots of steaming rice and monkey. Geist kept glancing at them, staring at their bare breasts.

The building was constructed of thatch-woven walls covered by a thatch roof. The floor was made from logs that had been stripped on one side so that they were flat. A large stone at the far end held ashes from cooking fires, and a hole in the roof over it let the smoke escape. There were no furnishings in the large hootch, no sleeping mats and personal articles. It suggested that the hootch was used by visiting tribesmen.

Tynan switched his attention to the man. He was

white, rather thin, and as dirty as the rest of the villagers. Tynan couldn't picture him either in an Army uniform or a three-piece suit favored by some of the CIA types he had known. The man seemed to be at ease with the natives, joking with the men and grabbing at the women, just as the local men did.

"These are the best women the tribe has to offer," said the man. "The youngest and prettiest. It is a sign of great respect that the chief sent them in."

Tynan looked at them and smiled at the one with long, jet black hair that seemed to have been washed and combed recently. She smiled back and held up the pot of rice.

"I would think," said Tynan, "if you could arrange airlift out of here, we'll report back to Saigon." He looked at the leaf that he had used as his plate. He had eaten all the rice that he cared to.

"There is no need for that. Your wounded man is in good condition. There is no sign of infection and he is resting comfortably. He'll be safe here, and there is nothing they can do for him in Saigon that we can't do here."

"But the mission is a bust," said Tynan. He thought about saying more, but decided against it. The man didn't have to know that his team was supposed to assassinate the NVA and VC leadership.

Then, as if the man had read his mind, he said, "There is no reason to cancel. You still have your special weapons. I have four fully trained strike companies here, each containing one hundred men. We can provide all the security you need while you complete your mission."

"I'm sure that there are other teams out," said Tynan quickly, without thinking.

"We don't know that. Your sergeant and you can

operate as the shooters, I can spot for one, and we
have a couple of men who speak passable English,
good French if either of you are conversant in that
language, who can spot for the other. And each can
have a company for security.''

Tynan shook his head. ''I don't think so.'' But
even as he said it he realized two things. One, the
man seemed to know what the mission was without
Tynan telling him—which meant he had been in
contact with someone in Saigon who was in the
know—and two, his own resistance to the idea was
that he was into the mindset that the mission should
be scrubbed. No reason for it if the replacements
were available, as the man said.

''Who are you?'' asked Tynan again.

''If you need a name, why don't you call me
John.'' He shook his head. ''My presence here is
even a bigger secret than yours.'' He smiled, almost
laughed. ''Security about this is stupid. Your mission
is a secret and you don't want to tell me anything.
Mine is a secret and I don't want to tell you anything. We sit here and dance around, afraid of breach-
ing security even though we both know that the other
won't talk and the other seems to know about the
mission.''

''You're right,'' said Tynan, ''but I'm not going
to tell you a thing.''

''No. And I'm not going to tell you.''

Geist stopped eating long enough to say, ''But I
will because I'm only a sergeant and don't understand the finer workings of all these security mat-
ters.'' He grinned at both of them but said no more.

John waited in silence for a moment and said,
''Then is the mission on?''

Tynan rubbed his chin. He didn't like working

with these people only because he didn't know them. But then the same could be said of Geist, except that he had picked up Geist on an official U.S. installation and knew something of his background. These people could be setting him up. But if that was the case, why go through all the trouble of organizing a mission? Why not just bring ten guys in and open fire?

No, John had to be some kind of deep cover, CIA operative, either civilian or Special Forces. With his help, Tynan could complete the mission. So why was he hesitating?

Tynan smiled to himself. Because he didn't like the idea of assassinating anyone. Before Sterne and Boone had been killed, Tynan hadn't had to be a trigger man. He had dodged that assignment. Now there was no choice and that was why he was hesitating.

"We've already lost one day," said Tynan, capitulating suddenly. "We should move out as quickly as possible."

John was on his feet. "I can have the strike companies formed in thirty minutes. Take another thirty minutes to brief the key men about the mission. Say we move through the gate in an hour and a half."

"What about Jones?"

"He'll be safe here. When the mission is completed, we can airlift all of you out."

"Wouldn't it be better to leave about dusk?" asked Geist. "Use the darkness and give us a chance to sleep. We've been up going on two days straight."

"How about two this afternoon?" said John. "You guys can rest and we can make some time with a good chunk of daylight left."

"Good," said Tynan.

"Then I'll arrange it," said John. "Ah, you want the female companionship?"

"I think," said Tynan, "that we need the sleep more. We won't be trampling on their taboos, will we?"

"No," said John. "They're used to my bizarre ways by now. They'll just think you're strange, but they'll accept your decision. There will be some whispering among the men about the weird behavior." With that he herded the women out of the hootch, leaving Geist and Tynan alone to get some sleep.

"You trust that guy?" asked Geist.

"I don't know. His story makes sense, and I was told there would be friendlies here. No one bothered to tell me about an American though."

"So we're going through with the mission?" said Geist.

"Yeah. No reason not to," said Tynan, not sure if he believed it himself.

8

The force gathered at the gate wasn't exactly what Tynan had expected. They were all wearing complete fatigue uniforms, right down to blackened combat boots and soft boonie hats. Each wore a rucksack that looked as if it had been modified to fit the smaller Asian body. They carried a variety of weapons, most of them from World War II. M-1 carbines with banana clips, pineapple grenades taped to their web gear, and a few carrying M-60 machine guns or M-79 grenade launchers. They stood in two straight lines, giving the appearance of competent soldiers waiting on the parade field for the general to inspect them.

At the head of one line stood John. He was dressed just like his army. The fatigues he wore were greener than those of the U.S. Army and had epaulets with the rosettes and bar of a Vietnamese colonel pinned to them. He had shaved, reavealing patches of very white skin on his cheeks and chin, and had cut his hair. It was now washed and combed. It was almost as if the man who had met them at the gate in a loincloth had been replaced by the soldier who stood there before them. He carried a CAR-15 like the one Tynan had been forced to leave behind, and wore a couple of bandoliers of M-16 ammo strapped across his chest.

As Tynan approached, John said, "How are you going to split this up?"

"Sergeant Geist is somewhat familiar with the terrain around here. He's worked operations close to the border a couple of times. Thought he would go out with one team and you and I would take the other since I have no idea about the area surrounding this village."

"No problem." John turned and pointed at one of the men, waving him over. The man wore the rank of a Vietnamese lieutenant pinned to his collar. "This is Lieutenant Nung. He will act as your spotter and second in command."

Geist nodded but didn't know if he was expected to shake hands. He waited to see what Nung would do and when Nung didn't offer a hand, Geist said, "You know how to spot?"

"I see officer and tell you. You shoot him."

Geist grinned. "Yeah, that's about it."

Tynan pulled his map out of his pocket, opened it, and held it so that Geist could see it. "You have an area where you want to operate?"

"If you don't mind, I'd like the area closest to the border. That way, if I get into trouble, I can escape to Vietnam and radio for help."

"You got any recognition codes?" asked Tynan.

"Yes, sir. Memorized them in Saigon before I went out with my team. They should still be good."

Tynan looked at John. "Anything you want to say?"

"Yeah. Sergeant, if you find it necessary to flee into South Vietnam, separate yourself from these men as soon as possible. I don't mean desert them, or take a chance of getting your ass shot off, but once in the clear, tell Nung to take them home. He'll get them back here."

"Understood."

"Nung," said John, "get your men ready. Point out, watch the noise discipline, and don't get trigger happy. And listen to this man. He knows what he's doing."

"I understand."

"Okay, then head out," said Tynan. "See you back here in a week or less."

Nung turned and shouted a command. Two men separated themselves from the column, trotted down the road until they were clear of the pungi field. Then they headed for the jungle, disappearing into the deep green of the vegetation. The column including Geist followed them, a couple of the men peeling off as flankers as soon as they could avoid the pungi stakes, and nearly a squad hanging back for a rear guard. John had done a good job of drilling them.

John said, "We'll give them twenty minutes and then follow. Our scouts haven't seen a sign of the VC or NVA in this area in the last couple of weeks. I mean right around the village here. But then you might have led them here."

"Your scouts didn't report us."

"Ah, that's where you're wrong," said John. "That's why you didn't see anyone moving around in the village until you came in."

The man kept surprising him. Every time he turned around, John was throwing a new wrinkle at him. First it seemed like a sleepy little village. But the defenses were tough and well hidden. Tynan had noticed a couple of well-disguised machine gun bunkers. The men seemed like a ragtag bunch of natives, but then turned out in two sharp-looking companies of strikers. Finally, John was admitting to an intelligence system that had eyes and ears in the jungle around him. It was becoming an impressive operation. Tynan hoped that John would be rewarded for the job he was doing.

John looked upward, into the deep blue sky that was marked by only a couple of white puffs. He wiped a hand over his forehead and then rubbed it on the front of his fatigue jacket, leaving a ragged stain.

"It's going to be a hot one in the open. Canopy'll keep the sun off us for a while, anyway," he said.

"Yeah," agreed Tynan. "Then it'll be like marching through a steambath while wrapped in wet towels."

"Nobody said it was going to be easy," responded John. "If it was, then everyone would want to do it and the pay would stink."

"Well, they can have my position."

John checked his watch and said, "Katu, take point. Go man. Hurry."

One of the tribesmen fell out and sprinted down the road, his feet kicking up little clouds of dirt as he ran. As he cleared the pungi field, the whole column moved without a command. John and Tynan fell into the center of it, in the break that looked like the division between two platoons.

The point man chopped his way into the jungle, veered to the east, and found a narrow trail that looked as if it hadn't been used for a while. The bush and grass were beginning to grow back over it. There were a couple of men just visible through gaps in the trees, the flankers who were fighting the jungle.

Occasionally Tynan could hear something from them, a quiet rustling of the vegetation. He had to concentrate to hear it and figured that the men could move in complete silence if the pace was slowed. Tynan figured that it was going to be a long, hot, afternoon.

The explosion at the head of the column caught him by surprise. Tynan's first instinct was to dive for cover as the small arms opened fire, but he saw the men of the column spinning, their weapons at their hips, shooting into the trees. The noise grew until it was a continuous roar, the men charging into the trees, some of them screaming at the tops of their voices.

Tynan hesitated and then followed the strikers. He leaped over a small bush and came face to face with an NVA soldier. The man swung the barrel of his weapon up, at Tynan. He blocked it with the butt of his own, twisting it, forcing it back, away from him. The enemy went with the motion as Tynan shoved him. Before the man could recover, Tynan hit him in the back with his rifle butt, and as the enemy collapsed to the ground, Tynan shot him once in the chest.

Tynan leaped over the trunk of a fallen tree and spun to the right. He saw two men in the dark green of the NVA and opened fire on them. Both went down in tumbling, bleeding heaps without firing a shot at him. Tynan moved to the left and dropped to one knee, his back to a thick palm.

He saw two strikers leap at a single VC dressed in black pajamas. The enemy soldier fired his weapon but hit neither of the strikers. The VC then tossed his rifle away and leaped to his feet. He threw his arms in the air, shouting something in a high, tight voice.

But he kept backing away, finally turning to flee. Both strikers opened fire at the same instant. Tynan saw the trees and bushes around the man shredded by the bullets, but he kept running. Finally he was hit once. He staggered two steps, reached out, grabbed at a tree, and then fell. The strikers riddled him then.

All around the firing was tapering off. There was a single crash, a muffled boom from a Chicom grenade. Tynan looked toward the sound and saw a tiny cloud of dirt expanding and climbing toward the canopy, barely visible in the light mist and half light of the jungle.

He got to his feet, moved to the right, but found only a single body of a dead NVA soldier. There were three bullet holes in his back. Two were small, neat holes with a little blood around them. The other was fist-sized and exposed bone and lung. Near the man's hand was a pistol. Tynan picked it up and slipped it into his pocket.

"Cease fire! Cease fire!" called a voice.

There were a few more scattered shots. Tynan moved back toward the pathway. John stood there, his rifle held at the ready, watching as a striker dragged the body of a VC from the jungle by the feet. The top of the dead man's head was missing and he was leaving a slimy trail of blood and brains behind him.

John moved to the dead man, looked at the face, and then turned as his men pulled the rest of the ambushers from the jungle. They quickly checked the bodies, ripping off the insignia, taking the wallets and papers, and gathering up the weapons and ammo so that the VC and NVA wouldn't be able to recover them. They found a radio of American manufacture and kept that.

Tynan approached him. "You got security out?"

"Squads at both ends of the trail and flankers beating the jungle looking for any stragglers. I think we got them all."

"You sure?"

"Not really. We didn't give them much chance. Might have been a couple who escaped to the rear."

Tynan looked at the dozen bodies on the trail. "Why'd they hit us? They didn't have the force to take us."

John shook his head. "They didn't have a choice. I think they would have let us go given the size of our unit, but one of our flankers stumbled over them and started the fight."

"We lose anyone?"

"Couple of wounded. We'll send them back with a squad to guard them."

"This really tears it," said Tynan. "I just can't get a unit into position without getting ambushed. Maybe it would be best to call it off. Head back and wait for Geist to return."

"Christ, Tynan. There is no reason to call off the mission. We beat off the ambush. Destroyed it. The enemy, even if they get a report about us operating in the area, won't know what we're going to do."

"We've been compromised," insisted Tynan.

"The mission hasn't." John turned, pointed at one of the strikers and said, "Get the point out. We've got to move."

Tynan watched the man head out. The strikers formed on the trail. They rolled the bodies off it, out of the way, concealing them in the bushes. A squad of men joined together at the rear of the formation. A couple of them had bandages around their arms or chests or legs. Each of the men there had two or three weapons. They carried their own, those of the wounded, and those taken from the bodies. A point man left them, heading back they way they had come.

"We're on the way," called John.

Tynan turned and fell in with the men. Again he wondered about his reluctance to carry on. It was as if he was looking for any excuse to cancel the mission. Granted, he would be within his rights to quit at that moment. He had lost half his men and was working now with a group he didn't know. They had been spotted by the VC and NVA. No one in Saigon would be able to fault his decision to quit.

But then he knew that he could continue. He had the weapon that Sterne had zeroed. He had security, and he had a spotter. The only way to make it better was if he had zeroed the weapon himself. He knew it would shoot true, but at long ranges, over half a klick or so, the difference between his and Sterne's style of shooting could make him miss. Of course, a badly wounded NVA leader wouldn't be able to lead an assault either.

He turned his attention back to the trail. They were still wrapped in the twilight of the triple canopy jungle. Sunlight just didn't have a chance to make it to the jungle floor. He could see the men in front of him, each of them becoming gray figures walking through a gray landscape. If there were bright light, the jungle would be alive with color. Now it was a washed-color photograph.

He wiped the sweat from his face and looked at the strikers in line behind him. They were moving easily, as if the environment didn't affect them. Their uniforms were as dry as they had been when they put them on. They didn't seem to know the ups and downs of the terrain, ignoring the inconvenience of walking over the rough ground of the trail.

Tynan was perspirating heavily, couldn't breathe easily, and needed a drink of his water. He smiled at them and tried to pick up his pace, pretending that he wasn't bothered by the heat and the humidity and the terrain.

An hour later, they fell out, off the trail. The strikers took up positions on both sides of the trail, facing in opposite directions so that they could cover for each other. It was a quick way to form a perimeter and another indication of the professionalism of the strikers.

John came back, found Tynan sitting between two of the strikers, watching the jungle. He crouched next to him and said, ''Thought we'd take a break for some chow. When we finish, we'll have about two, three hours of light left. We should be able to get close to the target. We can infiltrate under the cover of darkness.''

''I haven't seen the place yet,'' said Tynan.

''No matter,'' said John. ''I've been there a hundred times. I think I know the perfect place to set up. I know the exfiltration routes and where to put the security force.''

''All right,'' said Tynan. ''Have you been there since the enemy buildup began?''

''No. But I can guess where they're going to put their headquarters. Where they'll house the officers. I've studied their lifestyle long enough to guess what they'll do.''

''Then you have one other problem,'' said Tynan. ''I'm not sure how far my weapon will shoot accurately. I didn't zero it and it's been dropped once.''

Now John smiled. "Maybe you were right. Maybe we should call this off."

"You serious?"

"No. We've come too far now. We have to take it to the end even if that end isn't what we want."

"I bow to your judgment," said Tynan.

"Then we'll prepare to move out in ten minutes."

"I'll be ready."

9

Just like the night before, it was midnight when they reached their destination. They came out of the jungle on a slight ridge that overlooked the village. Or maybe it should have been called a town or city. Tynan crawled to the edge of the ridge and looked down into the blackness that was punctuated by a couple of electric lights and a dozen or more lanterns. He could see streets between buildings, some of them two or three stories tall, he heard the idling of a couple of engines that might have been trucks or cars or generators, and he could see a few figures walking around. He used his Navy binoculars to study the scene. On the far side of the town he could see a row of tents, a pale smudge against the blackness of the landscape. Near the center of the town he saw the tower of a pagoda that reminded Tynan of a shot tower he had seen as a kid.

John crouched beside him, watching everything. He leaned close and said, "Military formation on the other side of the town."

Tynan nodded and said, "I've got it. You'd think

they'd be a little more careful about the placement of it. Makes a very inviting target."

"If you're allowed to target it," said John. "When there is no danger from the American military or Air Force, then it really doesn't matter where you put it. You find a place to snipe from yet?"

Tynan again swept the town with his binoculars. The obvious place was the tower, but if it was a pagoda, he wouldn't be able to get near it, and all too often there was only a ground floor and no way to get to the top without a ladder. There were a half dozen buildings that would give him a clear field of fire into the tent city, but Tynan doubted that the higher-ranking officers would be living in the tents. They would have found accommodations in the town.

"If there was some way of identifying the head-quarters buildings. This ridge is fairly good, except there's too much of the town masked by the tall buildings. And too much of the tent city hidden by the town."

"So you want to go into the town?" asked John.

Tynan lowered his binoculars and stared at the man. "Want to? No. Have to? Probably. There's one tall building there, on the edge, that might be the perfect firing platform provided it's not a barracks or something like that."

"Okay," said John. He pulled up the sleeve of his fatigue jacket and checked the time. "We've got about four hours of darkness left. I suggest that we scatter a platoon along the ridge here as a rear guard. Take the rest of the men with us. Put three squads into the jungle and take one with us for security at the site."

Tynan put his binoculars away and rubbed his face. He could feel the stubble of his beard and the wetness of his sweat. His eyes burned from the lack of sleep, and if he wasn't careful he could feel his head spin. The lack of movement, sitting quietly in one place did that. He took a deep breath and realized again just how much he hated this assignment. Lie in wait and pick off someone at long range. Given the circumstances, he would have to use the sound suppressor. It would reduce the noise of firing his weapon to little more than a cough and could give them a chance to escape, or the chance to pick off a few more of the NVA. He didn't know how it would affect the ballistics of the weapon, but then, there were so many other problems that it would do no good to worry about the minor shit. He was surprised that Sterne hadn't fired a few shots through it since it had been supplied in the weapons kit, but then, they had been rushed.

"Give me five minutes to get the platoon set and then we'll start down," said John.

Tynan pointed to the left. "There seems to be a stream down there and a road that leads from the city. Might make a good escape route."

"Yeah," said John, but he wasn't listening to Tynan. He crawled off into the dark.

Tynan could hear him speaking quietly to someone nearby; there was a rustling of leaves and then silence. Tynan stared into the jungle behind him, but couldn't see anyone moving. Again he was amazed at the discipline and ability of the soldiers. They had been such a ragtag lot when he first saw them, but they had broken up the ambush with only a couple of men wounded, and they were now moving through the jungle only a short distance away, but Tynan couldn't hear them. At least he assumed that they were moving back there.

"I've got the men placed," said John as he returned. "You ready?"

Tynan moved back, away from the edge of the ridge, and got to his feet. "Yeah. I'm ready. As ready as I'll ever be."

"This should be fairly simple, until we get to the bottom of the hill. Then the old pucker factor ought to take over and make things a little more interesting."

"Right. Lead the way," said Tynan.

John moved off to the right, at the very edge of the jungle, using it to cover himself. Tynan could just make out his shape in front of him. He could see that there was one man with John, and when he turned, he could see a couple of the men behind him, but he couldn't hear them. He never heard them when they didn't want to be heard.

Tynan felt his way along, one hand out like a blind man searching for obstacles. In his other he held a walking stick that he had cut as he crawled away from the ridge, feeling his way along the uneven trail. He stumbled over roots and holes that he didn't see or detect. Once or twice he was slapped in the face by a branch hanging in the way, making a little noise. The men around him glided through the jungle, along the trail without a sound.

A few minutes later the patrol halted. Tynan could hear the bubbling of the stream. He moved from the trail, touched the side of a giant, smooth tree, and crouched hidden in the shadows and bushes, waiting.

John came toward him and said quietly, "This is the jumping-off place. I scattered a squad near the stream. There's a small bridge across the river and a road that leads into the jungle. My men are wiring the bridge to blow it, though I doubt that the destruction of it will slow the pursuit, if there is one, but it might irritate them later.''

''Fine.'' Tynan moved back to the trail and followed John to the edge of the road. They paralleled it for a while and then came to the edge of the jungle. There was an open field, almost fifty meters across. It was obvious that someone had cut back the vegetation several months ago to create a clear killing zone. There were now scattered bushes and long grass that swept upward to the first of the buildings. Tynan could tell that they were mud hootches with thatch roofs. Beyond them he could see structures that were made of brick, wood, and mud, many covered by tin.

Tynan took out his binoculars again and studied the scene in front of him. He could no longer see anyone moving along the street. The sounds of the engines had died away until a single diesel pulsated in the night. The lights that had been sprinkled around the village had been extinguished until there was only a lone lamp at the far edge of town. He could see no sign of sentries or guards but assumed they had to be there. Under no circumstances would he erect a camp without mounting a guard detail of some kind. Even in the World the military installations had guards.

John touched his shoulder and pointed at the sky. The sliver of moon that had helped them earlier was now dropping to the tops of the trees where it burned a bloody red.

''Twenty minutes,'' said John, ''and it'll be gone. Then we can make our move.''

''Terrific,'' said Tynan. ''Just terrific.''

He moved back, deeper into the vegetation, and used his binoculars, scanning the town slowly. Finally, in a door that bordered the road leading in, he saw a match flare, and in the brief, dim light, he saw a sentry. The man was sitting on the ground, leaning against the wall of the building, his rifle near him. It was an indication about the level of the training in the town. Lots of soldiers didn't understand the meaning of standing guard. They thought of it as a punishment. They thought of it as a make-work project because there was no need for guards at this camp. Tynan knew of several circumstances in the Navy where the mounting of the guard was a function of punishment. You didn't get the sharpest soldiers that way. You got the fuckups, and the guard sitting in the doorway smoking was an example of that.

Slowly it seemed to get darker. The defined shapes of the buildings in the town, the bushes in the field, faded until they blended with their surroundings. It meant that the moon was gone. Tynan glanced up and saw that a bank of clouds was moving in, obscuring the stars. It would make the job easier. Make it harder for the enemy to see them as they ran across the open field.

John appeared next to him and touched his shoulder. Tynan put his binoculars away and unslung his weapon. He watched John work his way to the edge of the jungle. The support squad spread out, right and left of him. Slowly, carefully, they left the trees, keeping low and moving like arthritic men. They eased forward, crouching next to bushes or dropping into the deep grass, none of them making a sound. They crept toward the town, using the cover, and even though Tynan knew they were there, he lost sight of them in the field.

He followed them, using their techniques and remembering everything that he had learned during his training. No rapid movements. Fluid, loose movements that could be a bush blowing in the breeze.

Smooth, easy movements that wouldn't catch the eye. Soft movements that wouldn't crush leaves to make rattling sounds or snap twigs.

In no time he stood in the center of the field and felt all alone. He had lost sight of everyone with him. He crouched near a large bush to catch his breath. He hadn't known that moving slowly was such hard work, and realized that it was a function of the place where he stood. He wanted to wipe the sweat from his face and hands but didn't dare make the extra unnecessary move. He could have used a drink from his canteen but knew he would need the water more during the day. Besides, the middle of the field was no place to be drinking water. He rested there, feeling the sweat trickle down his back and sides, and he shuddered. Not from the cold, but from waiting for the bullet from the imagined enemy sniper.

He stepped around the bush, bent at the waist so that he was barely four feet tall. He moved his foot slowly, rocking from the heel to the toe so that he could feel the ground with his foot. That way he wouldn't snap a twig or stumble over anything hidden in the grass. For an instant he was sure that there would be snakes around just waiting for him to step on them, and then remembered that most snakes hid during the night. It was too cold for them.

Too cold? With the humidity at a hundred percent and the temperature in the low eighties? Not likely. It was something else to worry about, but he forced it from his mind. If he let his brain get cluttered with a lot of unnecessary thoughts about snakes, he would surely make a mistake.

He kept moving, his eyes on his destination. It seemed to be receding. Each step did nothing for him. He felt the weight of his pack pressing into his spine and wondered why it was suddenly so heavy. He wanted to sit down to adjust it, and realized what he was doing. He was searching for an excuse to relax for a moment because it didn't seem that he would ever get out of the field.

And then he was next to a building. Right and left were the strikers who had been with him, hiding next to the walls, waiting for John to give them their next order.

Tynan glanced around the corner of the building, down an alley that smelled of undercooked cabbage, dead fish, and human waste. He could see the shimmering surface of a puddle of stagnant water.

Across the street there was a one-story building with a ripped awning over a porch lined by a broken-down mud wall. There seemed to be a large window in the middle of the structure and faint lettering above it. Tynan thought that it was some kind of shop, like the dozens that sprang up around the American bases in South Vietnam, offering everything from laundry to girls.

Again John appeared at his side and whispered. "Still nothing. We're going on in. We're using the pagoda as a rally point because it's near the building we want. That's if we get separated."

Tynan touched John's arm to signal that he understood. He then moved around the corner of the building and was nearly knocked down by the smell. He kept his back to the rough, mud surface of the structure. There was a wooden staircase, just three steps that led to a door. Tynan stopped and turned so that he could look up them, but the door was shut and there was no sound from the interior. A window set to the side was dark.

Across the alley, he saw John stop and look at the

door. He shook his head, telling Tynan that there was nothing inside. He pointed to the front.

Tynan eased around the steps, looked back, and still saw nothing. At the edge of the building, he halted again and got to the ground so that his body was lying parallel to the building. He looked around the corner.

The street was deserted. It was a mud pathway with deep ruts in the center. It seemed to slope to the sides, and there was a large pool of water standing in front of a hootch that had a partially collapsed tin roof blocking its entrance. A couple of bushes hid the fence along the road. There was a brightly painted bus parked next to it. Tynan couldn't be sure of the colors in the dark, but he knew it was bright given the riot of patterns that he could see dimly. From that direction he could hear the insistent hum of the generator. A couple of poles set at odd angles held swaying wires ten feet above the ground.

Tynan glanced to the left and John held up a thumb. He then pointed across the street and pumped his fist twice, telling Tynan that they should run across it.

Tynan nodded his understanding and watched John get to his feet. Tynan did the same, glanced at the empty street again, and nodded. Together they broke from cover, bent low, running for the protection of the structures across from them. Tynan hit the wall of one of the buildings, watching the street, but there was no indication that anyone saw them.

They moved between the buildings and came to another street. Opposite them was the pagoda. There was no one around it. Without a word Tynan worked his way across the street, aiming for a large palm in the center of it. He stopped there, saw no one, and ran for the door of the building. He hesitated a moment at the door, listening, but heard nothing from the inside. It seemed that the guards, if they were stationed around, were on the main roads leading into town.

John joined him. Tynan reached out and touched the door and felt it give under slight pressure. He looked back, saw that John had his weapon ready, and nodded. At that instant he threw open the door and dived through. John followed him inside.

Tynan lay on the floor for a moment, listening. He could see the vague outline of furniture, a desk or two, and a lone chair. He got to his feet and moved to the rear of the room, where there was another door. As he looked back, he saw John was up, covering him. Tynan opened the door slowly and discovered the stairway.

"John," he hissed.

In the darkness he saw the other man turn and head for him. John paused and whispered, "Couple of the strikers should be here shortly."

Tynan nodded and stepped into the stairwell. He looked up but could only see the dim shapes of the stairs as he stood at the bottom. There seemed to be a faint glow near the top, as if he could see the ceiling.

There was a sound and John was in the stairwell with him. "Go on up. Strikers will follow."

Tynan kept his back to the wall and started up the stairs, his weapon pointed upward at a forty-five-degree angle. He kept his feet near the wall, stepping in the center of the risers, so that they didn't make any noise. He reached one landing, looked upward, toward the next, listening and waiting. Waiting for a voice to call out a warning in Vietnamese or to open fire. But that didn't happen and the only sound he could hear was the breathing of the strikers following him up.

When he reached the top floor, he didn't know what to do. He had hoped that he would come out on the roof. That way he could circulate, check for the best firing locations, and get a feel for the terrain around him.

"What's the problem?" asked John.

Tynan stared into the dark and said, "We've reached the top."

"Then let's check out the floor. See what it's used for. If it's empty we might have found the perfect hiding place. Won't be exposed."

Tynan shrugged and reached for the doorknob. He twisted it slowly and shoved the door in. There was no groan from rusty hinges or scraping of wood on wood. The door opened and Tynan stepped through cautiously. He flattened himself against the wall and stared.

The whole floor seemed to be open. There were no walls or partitions. Although it was dark, the walls seemed to have windows spaced equally around, letting in a little of the outside light. They were squares of dark gray set in walls of black. There were posts, supports for the ceiling, set across the floor, which seemed to have litter on it—Papers, a box, broken bits of wood, and a large, white cloth. It didn't look as if anyone came up there very often.

"This looks perfect," said John.

"A little too perfect," said Tynan. "First place we look has the top floor deserted."

"Makes good sense," said John. "These people have abandoned the tops of all their buildings because of the threat of air raids. They want to be closer to the ground. I'd be surprised to find any of the top floors in this town occupied.''

''It's awfully open,'' said Tynan. He didn't mention that they had a large tent city scattered on an open plain, suggesting that they weren't too worried about air raids. There were probably a dozen reasons for the floor to be abandoned. And it was possible that it wasn't abandoned. It was possible that everything had been stripped so they could build what they wanted up there.

''What the fuck you want?'' asked John. ''We couldn't find a better place if we looked for a week and a half, for Christ's sake.''

''Nowhere for a defense,'' said Tynan. ''In the event that we're found.''

''If they find us, there won't be a whole shit lot we could do. I'll put a couple of the strikers on the door to hold it, but if big Chuck arrives and looks in, we've fucking had it no matter what we do.''

''Yeah,'' said Tynan. ''I guess you're right there.'' He moved across the floor and looked out one of the windows. He could see the street they had just crossed, the big palm tree, and the edge of town. By standing next to the wall, he had enough of an angle to see the road that led out of town. There was still no movement along the road, and none of the strikers reported running into any guards.

He crossed the floor, being careful not to make noise with his boots on the bare wood. Outside the back he could barely see the tent city of the NVA. From his position he could see a circle of tents in the center that reminded him of the headquarters buildings on military bases. He sat down, leaned his rifle against the wall, and pulled out his binoculars. He studied the enemy camp, but there wasn't enough

light to see anything important. He thought that he
could pick out a roving guard, and it seemed they
had a flagpole planted in the circle of tents, but that
told him nothing yet. Just not enough detail visible in
the dark. When the sun came up, he might discover a
sign that pointed to the headquarters. It would be
nice if the NVA and VC labeled everything as the
Americans insisted on doing.

"How long to sunup?" he asked, his voice seeming unnaturally loud in the confined area.

"Hour or so," said John.

"Okay. Seems to me that we'll want someone on
the door at all times and we'll want someone at each
corner looking out the windows, watching for the
enemy. Carefully, so they're not seen. The rest of the
men can sleep or eat, but I wouldn't let them move
around too much. Someone downstairs might hear
them and come up to check."

"I'll see to it," said John. "When you going to
start your shooting?"

"Well, there's the other problem. If I do it right,
we could probably get away with picking off a couple, three, four of these guys. With the sound suppressor, there won't be much noise. If I wait until it's
close to sunset, we'll have dark to help cover our
escape. That will also cover the fact that I'm shooting the officers."

"That means we stay up here all day with a fairly
large military force in the jungle around us that could
be discovered at any time."

"So how good are your boys?" asked Tynan.

"The VC won't stumble across them, if that's
what you're worried about."

"I'm not worried about that." Tynan slipped his
binoculars back into the case and took out his can-

teen. He drank from it, filling his mouth and sloshing
the water around before swallowing it. He almost spit
out the tepid water, but didn't want to waste it. He
did it three more times and then capped the canteen,
setting it on the floor next to his rifle. The water
tasted terrible but it washed the cotton from his mouth
and quenched his thirst. He wished that he had a
beer, even a warm one.

Tynan unbuckled his pistol belt and slipped his
pack from his shoulders. He unbuttoned his shirt,
pulled up his T-shirt for the cooling effect, and leaned
back, his head resting on his pack, which made a
large, hard, lumpy pillow. He stared up at the light-
colored and cracked ceiling.

"I'm going to grab a little sleep now. Wake me
when it's light if I haven't gotten up by then."

"No problem," said John.

10

Tynan woke about an hour later, covered with sweat. He was hot and uncomfortable and found it hard to breathe. The windows were now a bright gray, suggesting that the sun was about to come up. Tynan wiped his face with the sleeve of his fatigues and found that his uniform was soaked. It was as if he had stood in a shower while fully clothed.

He sat up and looked around him. He could plainly see the other men. A few were crouched near the weapons, watching the streets below them. Two sat near the door, listening for sounds in the stairwell. The rest of them were scattered around the floor, sleeping.

John sat in a corner, a cigarette cupped in his hand. Tynan found it strange that the man would smoke in that situation. But then he realized that he knew next to nothing about the man. He didn't even know his name.

Tynan wiped his face again and then turned. He slid to the right so that he could look out the window. He could now see the enemy camp quite well. There were a dozen, two dozen men moving around it. He reached to the left for his pack, dug out his binoculars, and began to survey the area. He could see the differences between the NVA and the VC. That was obvious because of the differences in the uniforms. Dark green fatigues versus the black pajamas. Detecting the officers was going to be a little bit harder.

There was a scrap on the floor next to him, and Tynan glanced at John.

"You're awake?"

"Yeah. Anything happening?"

John shook his head. "City's still dead. Couple of guys moving around on the street, and I saw a woman running toward one of the hootches like she was trying to get home before her husband woke, but nothing of interest."

Tynan turned his attention back to the enemy camp. "Getting hot in here already."

"Wait until the middle of the afternoon," said John. "It'll probably be like an oven. None of the windows open."

"Oh shit," said Tynan.

"Oh shit." John grinned. "I don't suppose you have a glass cutter with you."

"Didn't expect to need one."

"Well, your first round will break the window," said John.

Tynan lowered his binoculars and said, "The last thing I need to do is shoot through a sheet of glass."

"It shouldn't throw things off that much, should it?" asked John.

"Look. I'm firing a weapon that I've never shot before and didn't zero. I'm shooting from over half a klick and now I have to shoot through the glass in a window. No, it shouldn't throw things off, but it could."

"Don't get testy on me now," said John. "Hand me the binoculars and I'll see what's happening out there."

Tynan ducked back and sat down leaning against the wall. He gave the binoculars to John and watched as the other man crouched about two feet from the window so that he was well back in the shadows. It would make it nearly impossible for anyone outside to see him.

"Okay. Okay," he said. "Got a couple of wheels running around now. One's an NVA colonel, I think, and the other might be a general. A bunch of lieutenants and captains too. Yeah." He looked at Tynan and added, "There's a bunch of them here. Looks like it's some kind of flag-raising ceremony. Probably do it every morning. You sure you want to wait for dark?"

"You want me to take them now?"

"Why the fuck not? They're out there, most of the camp's asleep. We hit them and blow out of here."

Tynan moved to the window and looked out. "Which one's the general?"

John moved over so that his face was near Tynan's and he had the same viewing angle. He handed the binoculars back to Tynan and said, "Okay. You see the flagpole. Two guys standing alone by it. Bunch of guys standing behind them. One on the right is the general and the one on the left is the colonel."

"Yeah. Got it." He grabbed his sniper's rifle and popped the lens caps off the scope. He moved around and sighted through it. The two men loomed in front of him. He set the cross hairs on the chest of the NVA general who was saluting as if he was now a part of a flag-raising ceremony.

"Break the window," said Tynan.

"What?"

"Break the fucking window," Tynan shouted.

John glanced at the naval officer and then picked up his CAR-15 and used the metal butt plate on the glass. Almost as it shattered, Tynan fired. A slight cough as the sound suppressor did its job.

Tynan moved the weapon to the left and pulled the trigger again and then lowered it. He grabbed the lens caps and began putting them on the scope.

John watched the enemy. He saw the general stagger, clutch his chest, and fall to his side. The colonel turned and caught the second round in the stomach. He sat down, both hands on his abdomen, looking surprised and sickened. The men behind the two wounded officers hadn't moved and hadn't figured it out. They seemed to be staring upward at the flags.

"Both down," said John. "Can't tell if they're dead or not. No reaction. Now somebody's moving in. Here they go. People running all over the fucking place." He was grinning.

Tynan shouldered his pack and buckled his pistol belt. He glanced at the canteen, grabbed it and drained it, spilling some of the water down his chin. He jammed the empty canteen into its holder and moved to the door.

"Let's get out of here."

John clapped his hands once. Everyone was awake, waiting for instructions. John said something to them in their native language and the men leaped into action. The two at the door opened it, looked out, and disappeared through it.

The rest of them gathered near the door. John opened it and searched the landing just outside. The two advance men had gone down. John snapped his fingers, pointed, and two more men headed after them.

Tynan followed them, stepping out of the hothouse third floor. The change in temperature was unbelievable. Suddenly he was cool, relishing the light breeze that circulated in the stairwell. He nearly ran down the stairs, making a little noise. He stopped at the bottom, saw two men near the door, and exited. Two more men were near the front of the building, watching the street. Tynan turned and saw the rest of the men appear from the stairs.

From somewhere outside a siren sounded. Tynan turned to look but could only see the back wall of the building. He kept moving, hit the front wall, and waited. The two men there opened the door and sprinted into the street. They took up firing positions in the alleyways across from the building, guarding both the approaches. Two other men dodged out the door, splitting right and left, finding hiding places on that side of the street behind a mud wall and next to the trunk of a tree.

John came up behind Tynan and said, "We better scram. Sounds like someone tripped an alert siren."

"Street's clear."

"Then go. Take the alley and stop at the far end. Wait for us."

"Got it." Tynan leaped through the door and ran across the street. He ducked around a corner, past the striker, and continued down the alley. He dropped to the ground and studied the street, but saw no one on it yet.

Shooting broke out behind him. He turned and watched as John and four of the strikers came at him. They took up positions along the alley, watching for pursuit.

Tynan looked down the street and watched as three VC entered it, carrying AK-47s. Two of them peeled off and kicked in the door on one of the hootches. As they disappeared inside, Tynan popped the caps from his rifle's scope, letting them fall to the dirt. He sighted on the remaining soldier, placing the cross hairs on the center of the man's chest. He squeezed the trigger, felt the weapon jam into his shoulder, and heard the quiet pop of the round. The enemy jerked to the rear, throwing his weapon into the air. He dropped to the ground, rolled to his stomach, and looked as if he were trying to do a pushup. He collapsed into the mud and didn't move. Through the scope, Tynan could see the man's uniform suddenly turn a wet, rusty brown.

Tynan turned and sighted on the door where the other two had vanished. One of them reappeared, took a step out, and then hesitated, his eyes falling on the dead man. The second man leaped from the hootch, and as he passed the first one, Tynan shot him. The round exploded out his back, splattering the wall near him. As that man died, Tynan shot the last of the enemy. He saw the round punch through the material of the man's uniform, saw the spray of crimson and the expression of pain and surprise on the man's face.

"Let's go," said a voice behind him.

He glanced back and saw John. He leaped to his feet, checked the street again. Behind him there was more shooting, now coming from weapons other than AKs and SKS's. American-made carbines were firing. Most of it was single shot and not full automatic. There were sporadic bursts that ripped through the air.

"They've tumbled to us!" said John. "Go!"

Tynan stepped into the street and then ran across it. He hit the wall of the building and turned back to cover the men following him. He saw the strikers run from the alley and heard a burst of fire. Two of them went down, rolling over and then lying still. Behind them, Tynan saw an NVA soldier—a big man wearing a pith helmet, running after them, the bayonet on his AK extended. He stopped over the body of one of the strikers. Tynan aimed and fired. The man jerked upright as if suddenly burned. He looked right at Tynan and tried to lift his weapon to fire it. Instead he fell to his knees. He reached up to touch his wound as he toppled forward, into the mud.

In the alley, behind the dead NVA soldier, several more enemy appeared. They leaped into hiding places, using the side of the building, the broken-down mud wall, and an overturned ox cart for cover. They opened fire, pouring out rounds. Tynan watched the side of one of the buildings shattered under the impact, the dirt and debris cascading to the ground. There was a shout, a scream actually, and then an explosion from a grenade.

"We've got to go," said John.

"Everyone accounted for?" asked Tynan.

"They know the plan for exfiltrating. If they get separated from the main group, they are to get out the best way they can. If they reach the jungle, the bad guys won't be able to catch them."

There was a short burst of fire and a line of AK rounds stitched across the wall above them. John ducked, looked up, and then said, "Come on."

Tynan ran down the alley and slid to a halt. He was facing the open field. Fifty yards of open ground that they had to cross to reach the safety of the jungle. Tynan hesitated, heard two more grenades detonate behind him, heard the shrapnel bouncing off the side of a hootch, and glanced at John. Three of the strikers jumped to the left and spun, facing the way they had come. They opened fire, hosing down the alley. At that moment, Tynan sprinted from the alley and into the open. In front of him, at the edge of the jungle, he could see a couple of the strikers who had stayed back, by the bridge. They were preparing to cover the withdrawal.

As he got halfway across the field, he heard an AK open up. There was a sound near his head like angry bees. In front of him, he saw a striker get to his feet and fire back. Tynan zigged to the right, leaped high over a bush, stumbled, and then regained his balance. He crossed the rest of the field in a sprint and then dived into the jungle as the striker poured a steady stream of fire back into the town.

He rolled to his shoulder and came up on his knees. In the field were five or six of the strikers. A VC appeared at the mouth of the alley, standing there, his knees locked, aiming. Tynan threw his weapon to his shoulder, sighted, and fired. The man dodged to his right, apparently unharmed. Tynan picked him up again, sighted, and shot. The round blew the top of his head off, flipping him back.

Now the jungle around him erupted as the strikers found targets. Several NVA and VC appeared at the edge of the town. The ground and buildings around them exploded under the fusillade. They dived to the rear, out of the way.

"Withdraw," ordered John in English. Then he shouted something in the local dialect and the shooting died.

With that, Tynan ran to the rear. He paralleled the road, keeping to the vegetation until he reached the stream. He leaped down, into it, waded across, the water lapping at his thighs, and entered the trees on the other side. As he did, he saw two of the strikers run for the bridge.

Tynan saw John and angled toward him. Before he could say a thing, John yelled, "To the ridge. Withdraw to the ridge."

At that moment there was a loud, flat bang. Tynan saw the bridge disappear in a cloud of black smoke and red dust.

The shooting increased again. This time it came from the ridge above them. Tynan stopped near the trunk of a teak tree. He turned, and through the vegetation he could see the VC and the NVA swarming across the open ground, attacking toward the ridge line. A heavy machine gun opened up ripping into the jungle, shattering tree trunks, and smashing into the earth. Tynan could see the muzzle flashes tucked into one of the structures bordering the open ground.

Tynan stepped back and braced his rifle against the tree. Through the scope he could see a shadowy shape inside the building behind the machine gun. He centered the cross hairs and pulled the trigger. A second later the machine gun fell silent. Tynan grinned.

From the area where the bridge had been, there was a wild burst of firing. Tynan saw three of the strikers at the edge of the stream shooting into a platoon of VC who were rushing down the road, supported by an armored car. As he watched, the car slid to a stop in a cloud of dust and two machine guns opened fire, raking the bank and the stream, the water splashing ten, twelve feet into the air. The three strikers went down, one of them rolling into the water, staining it bright red.

The VC then rushed the stream bank, trying to outflank the men on the ridge by coming up beside them while the NVA assaulted the front. Tynan sighted on them, picked out the officer who carried a pistol and wore a uniform instead of black pajamas, and fired at him. The man stumbled forward and fell into the water not far from the dead striker.

Tynan shifted and fired again, but missed. The bolt of his weapon locked back. He hit the magazine release, let it fall, and snatched another from his ammo pouch. He slammed it home, released the bolt, and sighted. He dropped another of the enemy soldiers.

As it appeared that the VC would be successful in their flanking maneuver, more shooting erupted in the trees. The VC caught in the open near the bridge and along the banks of the stream began to fall. There was a halfhearted surge into the water that broke under the firing.

Tynan lowered his rifle and ran up the hill, using the dense jungle vegetation for protection. He reached the crest behind a line of strikers. They were pouring intense fire into the charging NVA. Tynan could hear some of the strikers shouting at the enemy, taunting them. He dropped to a knee and began shooting at the enemy soldiers. He searched for the officers, identifying them by their collar tabs and their weapons. He shot one of them and watched the man fall. The enemy tried to get to his hands and knees, his head down as if looking at his knees. With one hand he searched for his pistol.

"Prepare to fall back," said John. "First, third, and fourth sections, withdraw. Second section, keep up the firing." He followed that with a command in a foreign language. Tynan figured that he was telling him the instructions before he gave them to the strikers.

Tynan watched as most of the men retreated, crawling to the rear until they were protected from the enemy bullets by the jungle and the ridge line. Below him, in the open field, he could see the bodies of thirty or forty of the VC and NVA. The rest of them had dropped back, to the protection of the buildings on the edge of the town.

As the men broke contact, they formed into a double column. Two men ran ahead, taking the point, and more peeled into the jungle as flankers.

"Let's get out of here," said John.

Tynan retreated from the edge of the ridge where he could see what was happening. He stopped long enough to watch the rear guard. They were firing into the town, their weapons on full automatic. Two grenadiers were launching 40mm grenades, both HE and Willy Pete. The white phosphorus exploded into fountains of flaming debris that spread fire across the edge of the field and among the buildings. Black smoke poured from the top of one of the structures and flames appeared behind one of the windows.

Tynan spun and ran after the men of the column. As he did, he thought about the bridge and realized that it hadn't been blown. The strikers had been killed before they had a chance to touch off the explosives. They were jogging along a trail, putting distance between them and the enemy village. John was in front of him, running along the column, urging the men on, telling them to run, to get out, and they would hit the NVA and VC in another place at another time. They would have another chance to kill the enemy. But they had to get clear.

As he ran, Tynan could hear the shooting behind him tapering off as the strikers of the rear guard attempted to withdraw. There were more explosions, some of them from Chicom grenades that had to fall far short. The heavy machine gun began to hammer again, its bullets smashing into the trees and bushes, stripping them and destroying them.

Ahead of him, Tynan saw the column spreading out, the point getting too far in front. John was there, waving and shouting, forcing the men to move with a combination of their own language and English. When one man fell to the side of the trail, his breath coming in ragged gulps, John was there, jerking on the straps of his rucksack. The man looked up, sweat pouring from his face. He tried to flop back, but John lifted him to his feet and kicked him in the butt. When it looked as if the man was going to fall again, John slapped his face and shoved him forward. The man began to move, his pace slower than the rest of the men, but he was moving. Staggering forward, but following the rest of the patrol.

Tynan ran by him, wishing that they could stop for a moment. He wanted to take a drink of water as cotton formed in his mouth and pain began radiating through his chest because of the strain of running through the humid heat of the jungle. If he could only rest for a moment. Just a chance to catch his breath. To stop the pain inside. But he knew that they couldn't stop for a while. They needed to escape from the VC and the NVA who would soon be searching for them. If the enemy officers ever got their men moving again. If the officers felt the urge to try it, now that some of the senior men had been killed.

Then, from far to the rear came a wild burst of sustained firing. AK and SKS against M-1 and M-16. Detonations of grenades and the rattling of machine guns. A firefight that started with a couple of shots that built until it was the continuous roar of a pitched battle. The rear guard was doing its job, and probably dying doing it.

But the pace of the column didn't slow. John kept them moving, running up and down, pushing and yelling until they reached a hill that grew from the floor of the jungle. The men detoured, climbing rapidly until they were at the top. They spread out forming a perimeter at the top, guarding all the approaches.

John stood in the center, his forearm against the trunk of a tree and his head down, breathing rapidly. Sweat dripped from the tip of his nose and chin, falling to the dark, moist earth beneath him.

When Tynan got near him, he said, "I don't think they'll follow."

"Why the fuck not?" said Tynan between gasps as he tried to catch his breath.

"They got the rear guard and they'll be happy with that. They won't want to chase us through the jungle so they'll pretend they got everyone."

"But they didn't even come close," said Tynan.

"Doesn't matter. They got enough guys to save face and can tell each other how brave they were. They won't follow."

"You're that sure," said Tynan.

"I'm that sure."

11

They had been sitting quietly on the hilltop for nearly an hour and there had been no sign of pursuit. There was no noise from the jungle, no more firing, and no sign of the rear guard. It seemed that John had been right about that. The NVA had overrun them and was happy with the imagined victory. Tynan wasn't sure that he approved of the philosophy, but knew that the rear guard rarely survived the task. It was their job to stop the enemy even if it meant they didn't get clear.

Tynan sat in the center of the perimeter, leaning against the smooth trunk of a teak tree, checking the sniper rifle. He had changed magazines, figuring on using the partial for his last if it came to that. He examined the mounting bolts for the telescope and could see that they were still tight. He wanted to put the caps back on, but had dropped them somewhere near the bridge.

John dropped to the ground near him. He had out a map that was covered with French writing. He folded it until it was a square about a foot across and he held it so that Tynan could see it clearly.

"I make it about twenty klicks to the next site," said John.

"Twenty klicks to what next site?"

"The next place where we can expect some kind of buildup by the enemy. You see this ville here? It's only a couple of klicks from the Ho Chi Minh Trail. Given the light jungle between the trail and the ville, the fact there is an unimproved road that leads to it, and it has a population of five or six thousand, I would expect the NVA to be hanging around there. That makes it the perfect target for us."

Tynan let the bolt slam home and flicked on the safety. He turned, looking at the tree, thinking that he would lean his rifle against it, but then decided to hang on to it. He stared John in the face and said, "I would think that we've done enough. We disrupted the men in the town. And we lost a good fifteen or twenty men ourselves."

"We have the opportunity to do more," said John. "We can stir up the pot a little. See what we can do to cause more trouble for the bad guys."

Tynan shook his head. He was going to make a flip remark about armchair commandos, although John was in the field with him so that it wasn't a fair comment. And then he had another thought. This man seemed to know more than he should have. He seemed to be tuned into the wavelengths on which the NVA and VC operated. He was more than just a training officer for the local population. There had been no evidence of radio equipment in John's village, but the way the man leaped into the assignment suggested that he knew more than he was letting on. Besides, if he did have radio equipment, he would have kept it hidden anyway. It wouldn't be good for there to be antennae sticking up all over the place.

"I have one question," said Tynan, "and I want a straight answer. Who the fuck are you?"

John looked at the men on the perimeter. He looked at the three men near one tree. Two with grenade launchers and the third with a rifle. And then he looked back at Tynan.

"I haven't answered that question for anyone in the last six months."

"I don't give a fuck about that," said Tynan. "Before we go on, I want to know who you are and who you're working for and what the fuck you're doing out here."

"Why do you keep trying to abort the mission?" countered John. "I've had to push you into everything since you arrived at the front gate of my camp."

"Because from the moment I arrived, I've been in trouble. I wouldn't have come to your village if there hadn't already been complications to the mission. Rather serious complications at that."

"But you've been dragging your feet even after I explained that we could pick it up. Now you want to call it off again because we've taken a few casualties."

Tynan laughed and shook his head. "Nice try. Nice fucking try, but you still haven't answered my question."

"All right. I'll level with you. I work for the CIA. We've been arming and training the locals for a couple of years. Figure that we can get them to fight the communists, stop some of the traffic on the Ho Chi Minh Trail, and take the pressure off the Saigon government. Of course, since Laos is a neutral country, we have no one operating in it."

"Of course," said Tynan.

"And I know that taking out some of the top leadership is going to slow down or stop any threat from this buildup. Now that I've told you that, why don't you want to continue it?''

Tynan glanced at the sniper rifle and said, ''Because I'm not convinced that this is all that effective. I'm not convinced that assassination is the proper way to fight a war.''

''Oh,'' said John sarcastically. ''There's a proper way to fight a war? I thought you just killed as many of the enemy as you could, while destroying his capacity to wage war. When the cost got too great for him, he quit. Or when it got too great for you, you quit.''

''And you're right,'' conceded Tynan, ''except that we're not killing the enemy like that and we're not destroying his capacity to wage war. We're just jacking around losing people, and this mission seems to underscore that. I smoke a couple of field-grade officers we think might be important and lose twenty guys in the process. Doesn't seem worth it.''

''This isn't the place to debate the policies of the war,'' said John.

''No. It isn't,'' agreed Tynan.

''Okay,'' said John, pointing to his map again. ''We could be here near dark. Give us a chance to scope out the situation.''

Tynan had to grin. ''Don't give up, do you?''

''Not when there is a job to be done.''

''All right,'' said Tynan, ''show me what you've got.''

They ate a cold meal on the hilltop, giving any survivors of the rear guard a chance to find them. No one ever showed up. John thought that they might have tried to make the camp, if they had gotten away. He didn't expect to find any of them there either.

When they finished eating, they buried the remains of the meal in the soft, moist earth and began to filter off the hill. They had a point out about a hundred meters, a squad following him. There were flankers out. John was taking no chances on walking into another ambush.

With twenty klicks to cover, the pace had to be fairly steady. They moved into the jungle, hacking their way through the undergrowth using machetes. It was slow, hot work that meant the point man had to be rotated frequently. Tynan didn't like the noise that they were making, but if they slowed to maintain noise discipline, they would make only a couple of hundred meters an hour.

And then they broke through the thickest of the jungle. The point man stood in the center of a trail. Dark, wet dirt in the middle, light grass at the sides, and then deep, dark green vegetation all around it. It was almost like standing in the center of a living tunnel.

John caught him a few minutes later. He sent men down it in both directions, telling them to search for signs that someone had used it recently. Signs that someone might be using it now. He spread the rest of the men in the jungle, told half of them to guard the other half and then change in ten minutes. When everyone was settled, he took a drink from his canteen and watched Tynan do the same.

Within twenty minutes they were moving again, along the trail. Since they were in Laos, the VC and NVA didn't booby-trap anything and rarely set up ambushes. Most of the fighting was in South Vietnam, and the enemy didn't worry about attacks in Laos. The Americans weren't allowed to operate there and the South Vietnamese wouldn't.

Using that logic, John determined that it would be safe to follow the trail. Tynan pointed out that he was taking a lot for granted, but John told him that in time of war, a commander had to take some chances to win.

Tynan watched John head toward the point and decided that he didn't like being lectured on what it was like to fight a war. He had been doing it for a couple of years and had an idea about it. But he didn't say anything. He just fell into the line and followed the man in front of him as they nearly ran along the trail.

They spent the whole afternoon moving through the jungle. They stopped twice to rest and drink water. Finally, John halted them momentarily and then ordered them to turn to the right. They entered the jungle on line, moving to the east. Within minutes they stopped again. Through gaps in the vegetation, Tynan could tell that they had reached the edge of the town.

Tynan veered to the right so that he was standing next to John, listening to the roar of truck engines. He could see a cloud of smoke rising above the buildings. He stared at it, realizing that it was the North Vietnamese Army operating as if they were on maneuvers in friendly territory. Trucks driving around, troops marching. The only thing they were missing was air support, and he knew that they wouldn't get it. It had been years since the MiGs of the North Vietnamese Air Force had strayed into foreign lands. They stayed over North Vietnam and sometimes engaged the American fighters and bombers during raids. Only rarely did the MiGs venture into Laos.

John was standing next to a tree, a pair of binoculars in his hand as he surveyed the town. As Tynan approached him, he handed them over.

''Take a look.''

Tynan lifted the instrument to his eyes. They were only slightly above the town, so he didn't have much of an angle on it, but that didn't matter. He could see down one of the streets, a street bordered by one-story buildings made from mud and thatch and wood. He could see a hundred soldiers lining the street as if they were part of an honor guard, each man with a new looking AK-47 and dressed in a dark green uniform. Each of them wore a khaki-colored pith helmet. It was as if they were spying on a parade.

''What the fuck?'' said Tynan.

''I don't know,'' said John. ''Looks like some wheel is about to arrive.''

Tynan swept his gaze over the rest of the town. He could see a number of jeeps on side streets and there were a couple of cars, French Citroëns, one with North Vietnamese flags on the front fenders.

There were civilians on that street, nearly a hundred men and women dressed in their finest holding either a North Vietnamese flag or the flag of the National Liberation Front. There was something about them though. Something that didn't look quite right, as if they weren't happy about being on the street holding those flags. It might be some kind of arranged spontaneous demonstration, like those the Soviets arranged in satellite countries.

Tynan looked up at the tops of the buildings and saw a dozen soldiers there. Most held AKs but there were a couple of heavy machine guns with the sights used for antiaircraft weapons. He thought two or three of the men carried SA-7s, the shoulder-fired antiaircraft missile. It was as if the NVA had something in the town that they wanted to defend. Something important.

"What the fuck is going on here?" asked Tynan again. "You have any idea?"

"I think we've stumbled onto the tactical head-quarters for the invasion into the South," said John. He crouched and pulled out his map, moving slowly and carefully as if afraid that he would give away their position just by being there.

Tynan turned and looked over his shoulder. There was a highway that led directly into South Vietnam that connected with Highway Fourteen. It was just as he had been briefed in Saigon. By running up the road to the north they would end up in Da Nang, and to the south they would roll through Kontum. All that put them in a position to cut the country in half. Tynan could see the whole plan on his map as if it were a history lesson being diagrammed in a high school class. It was so simple and so obvious.

"That would mean the main leadership is right here," said Tynan.

"I wouldn't be surprised," said John.

Tynan glanced at the sniper rifle. "Then a couple of well-placed rounds could easily take out the top man."

"If we can spot him," said John.

"I would imagine that he's the one with the car and the flags on the fender."

John looked up from his map. "I would think so."

"Then we've got him," said Tynan.

John folded his map and stuffed it back into his pocket. He rubbed a hand across this face and wiped it on the front of his uniform, then stood up and took his binoculars from Tynan. He studied the streets until he found the cars that Tynan had mentioned.

"Sweet mother of Jesus," he said. "We've got us

a real live leader of the North Vietnamese here. My God, I just don't fucking believe it.''

"You see him?'' asked Tynan.

"Not yet, but I know who it is. I don't believe it, but I know who it is. The plan sounds just like something he would design. Cut South Vietnam in half.''

Tynan slipped off the safety of the sniper rifle. He eased to the left, searching for a better firing position. One where he had an unobstructed view of the cars.

"You going to let me in on the secret?''

John lowered the binoculars and looked into Tynan's eyes. "What we have here is the man who engineered the attack on the French forces at Dien Bien Phu. The man who was responsible for defeating the French, although his master plan was to keep throwing troops into the battle until he won. Not a great military strategy, but one that worked at the time. Probably is why we're having the big buildup now.''

Tynan felt his stomach turn over and his head spin. "Christ! You don't mean Giap.''

"The one and only. General Vo Nguyen Giap, top military leader in North Vietnam.'' John stopped talking, turned and looked back at the cars. "Do you know what it would do to the morale of the North Vietnamese if we could pick his ass off? It would be a blow that would knock them for a loop. Maybe make them negotiate in earnest.''

"Yeah,'' nodded Tynan. "This one would be worth it, if we get the chance.''

"We'll get it,'' said John. "All we have to do is be patient and we'll get it.''

"Maybe we should tighten the lines a little. Tell the men to be careful and not to move.''

"Don't worry about the strikers. They'll be fine. All we have to do is find you the best firing platform so that you can make the shot. And then we'll have to fade real fast or we'll all die."

Before Tynan had a chance to reply, there was a burst of fire from an AK-47. Tynan jumped at the sound and turned toward it, but couldn't see anything.

John laid a restraining hand on his arm and said, "Might mean nothing. Might mean that one of the VC got trigger happy for no reason. Maybe shooting at a snake. Maybe just an accident."

But there came a second burst, followed by the detonation of a grenade and then the sound of an American-made M-1 carbine firing single shot. It was answered by two AKs and then a long burst from an RPD machine gun. That ignited the firefight. More weapons joined in and it was suddenly apparent that a North Vietnamese patrol had stumbled over the left flank of the strikers' force.

"Shit," said Tynan. "That tears it."

"No," said John. "We can still get Giap. We'll just have to be a little clever about it."

12

As the shooting broke out on the left, Tynan watched the town, waiting for a reaction from the force there. More strikers were joining the fight, and the sound of the battle increased until it was a roar.

In the town, everyone had disappeared. The soldiers were no longer standing guard. The people were no longer waiting for a parade. On the tops of the buildings, the antiaircraft machine guns had disappeared, pulled back out of the line of fire. A minute later they began hammering the tree line from the second-story windows.

More of the strikers began to fire until the whole line was engaged. Tynan could see the VC and NVA scurrying around, some behind the windows of the structures, others dashing between buildings, searching for hiding places. From the windows came the sparkling of muzzle flashes that were barely visible in the late afternoon sun.

There was a series of pops, and mortars began to crash into the jungle around them.

"Fucking gooks," yelled John. "Mortars are fucking worthless in the jungle."

The shooting from the town slowly began to increase as more of the NVA got into positions where they could shoot into the jungle.

Over the noise, John yelled, "You think you can get a shot at Giap?"

"Christ! From where? I stick my head up and somebody's going to blow it off."

"Yeah, but can you get him?"

"No. He's not going to show his face. You give me a target and I'll hit it, but I don't get the target, I can't shoot it. Giap's going to be kept inside."

From the town came the sound of bugles. The machine guns kept hammering and hammering and the mortars rained down, blowing holes in the soft earth and ripping at the vegetation. There was a surging charge across the open ground, the NVA pouring from the streets, the buildings, and their cover, shouting and shooting, running straight at the sliver of jungle where Tynan and the strikers waited.

Tynan watched as the front line of enemy, dressed in the dark green of the NVA, rushed him. Several of them dropped to the ground, rolling over, screaming in agony. Others took their places, sprinting for the safety of the trees. As it looked as if the enemy would make it, would overrun the strikers and kill them, the firing stiffened and became more accurate. A dozen of the enemy dropped, two dozen. They fell in heaps, blood staining their uniforms rusty brown, their bodies ripped by the rifle fire.

Tynan used his sniper rifle, aiming at the leaders, the men carrying the pistols, just as he had earlier. He saw one head fly apart. The body collapsed to the ground in a spray of crimson and a splash of gray.

"They're going to overrun us," Tynan shouted.

John, who was kneeling near him, his weapon on full auto, yelled back, "Not yet. Not yet."

The enemy line wavered a few feet short of the tree line. One or two of them penetrated it, but they were cut down immediately, their bodies riddled.

At that moment there was a single, piercing bugle call. The enemy suddenly broke the attack, retreating. As they cleared away, shooting from their hips, trying to get back, out of the way, the mortars began again. They fell close to the trees, providing cover for the fleeing NVA.

"They'll be back," said John.

Tynan glanced at him and thought he sounded as if he were in a bad western. "Maybe we should just try to fade out of here," he said.

"I want Giap."

"But we're not going to get a chance at him now. They're going to keep sending people at us until they either overrun us or force us out of here. Until they kill us all, and then Giap will drive out and look at the bodies."

"Look, we can't get into a running gun battle with these guys. They hold the cards. They have us outnumbered. We try to pull out, they're going to catch us in the open and cut us to ribbons."

Tynan turned and looked at the field. There were forty or fifty dead men lying out there. Mortars still fell, some of them among the wounded, but the shells were short of the tree line, as if trying to screen the men there from the town.

The firing from the left flank had tapered off until it was sporadic shooting. The machine guns hidden in the buildings kept pounding the trees, but most of the rounds passed harmlessly overhead.

"I think we'd better get out," said Tynan.

"I want Giap."

"You're not going to get him. Not now. You're sacrificing these guys for no reason."

John looked at him for a second. "Then why don't you just get out. Take the men and get out."

"What?"

"Give me that rifle. I'll stay here and see if I can't get a clear shot at Giap. You take the men and lead the bad guys out of here."

At that moment there was a whirring overhead and a crash that seemed to wipe out all sound around them.

"Shit. They've got artillery."

"Then there is no way that we can defend this position," said Tynan. "We've got to get out."

"You're right. Give me that rifle and get the fuck out of here."

"That's a—"

"Don't argue," snapped John. "There isn't time."

"We've all got to go."

"No! If you take all the men and try to get out, the bad guys might follow you. Overlook me. I lay low, wait for my chance, and then smoke Giap."

There was another explosion from an artillery round to the right of them. Tynan flinched as it detonated and could hear the dirt and debris rain down. He thought about what John had said earlier. That they couldn't afford a running gun battle, but now he was telling Tynan to do just that. It was a contradiction that Tynan didn't like.

"They've about got us bracketed. They'll be firing for effect in a couple of minutes and then sweep through here to pick up the pieces," said John.

"You've got to lead—"

"Nung can help. He speaks English." John turned,

saw the striker near him, and said, "Nung, I want you to listen to the lieutenant here. Get the men out."

"I understand," said the striker, nodding gravely. He might not have understood what was being said between John and Tynan, but did understand the order.

"You obey his orders like they're mine."

"Yes, sir."

"Okay, Tynan, you've got a lull here. You better get the fuck out or it's going to look like Custer at the Little Big Horn."

The firing from the machine guns had tapered off. There was a distant boom as if a single field piece had been fired. Again there was a whirring over them and the explosion behind them. They could hear the dirt and debris raining down through the trees.

Tynan looked at John, a man he had known for only hours, a couple of days at the most. A man whose real name he didn't know. But a man who wanted to stay and sacrifice himself in an attempt to kill Giap. Take out one of the top NVA leaders. It seemed a ridiculous thing to do, but then that's what heroes did. Stayed when it made no sense. And if John got Giap while Tynan was running through the jungle, the NVA pursuit would probably collapse.

"Okay, Nung," said Tynan. "Tell the men to start retreating. Fall back about a hundred meters and then collapse toward the center of the line."

Nung nodded and ran off, dodging about the trees, giving the instructions in a quiet voice, ducking behind trees, waiting for the enemy machine gunners to walk the bullets somewhere else, and then running off again.

Tynan handed the rifle to John. "I find that it pulls

slightly to the left. An inch or so at three hundred, four hundred yards.''

''Got it.''

''We'll make a little noise getting out. Let them know we're running.''

''Thanks.''

There was more that Tynan wanted to say, but he couldn't find the words. He hadn't given instructions to men who were about to commit suicide before. He was sure that was what John was doing, and he wasn't sure that he understood it, but he didn't have the time to argue about it. They had already wasted a couple of minutes debating it. Tynan had once told his men that strategy conferences in the field usually resulted in dead men.

Tynan saw the strikers working their way to the rear, fighting the jungle, trying to get out. He stared John in the eyes and said, ''Good luck.''

''Yeah. You too.''

Tynan picked up the weapon that John had been using and took a bandolier of ammo from him. He took off after the strikers, stopped, and looked back. John was standing near a large tree, looking up into the foliage on the branches. Another artillery shell exploded, this one short.

At the edge of the jungle, Tynan came to the strikers. Nung had gotten them spread into a defensive ring. He could see that several of them were wounded, the blood staining their uniforms. The faces of others were white with fear. They held their weapons in death grips, their knuckles white.

''Nung, let's get a point out. Head zero-nine-zero degrees. You got a compass?''

''Yes.''

''Good. Give it to one of the men and get him

moving. Get a couple of flankers out, no more than ten meters, and I want a squad as a rear guard.''

''Yes.''

''Then go! Go.''

Nung pointed at three of his strikers and rattled off the instructions. He gave his compass to one of them and the man trotted forward, disappearing into the vegetation.

Behind them Tynan could hear the mortars and artillery falling into the jungle, punctuated by the steady drumming of the heavy machine guns. They were far enough away that they were no longer in danger from it, and he couldn't see any of the explosions.

''Nung, let's get out of here. Everyone keeps moving. Keeps chugging along. I'll hang back with the rear guard.''

''Yes.''

Tynan watched Nung get the men moving again. He had to kick one or two of them who wanted to hide in the bushes and pretend that they were safe. As they moved out, Tynan checked his weapon, an M-1 carbine with a banana clip. He glanced at the men with him, pointed his weapon in the air, and opened fire, emptying it. The strikers with him didn't understand what he was doing and he couldn't tell them that he was trying to help John. Trying to let the VC and NVA know that they had withdrawn.

The artillery barrage had tapered off. The mortars still fell, and the machine guns still raked the tree line. The bugles came again and Tynan could hear the shout from a hundred, two hundred throats. It meant that another attack was about to be launched.

Tynan tapped the shoulders of the men nearest to him and pointed into the jungle. The men looked at him, not understanding what he wanted. Tynan grabbed one by the shoulder, jerking him to his feet and shoving him after the main body of the patrol. The others understood that immediately. They all fled, running as fast as they could.

Tynan dropped the magazine from his weapon, jammed another one, taken from the bandolier, into the rifle, and cranked off a couple more rounds. There was sound from the jungle, shooting from AKs, shouting from there in Vietnamese, bugles urging them on.

For a moment, Tynan hesitated. Then, deciding that the NVA had to know that the strikers were gone, he turned and ran after them. He caught them as they forded a shallow stream, half the force on one bank covering with the others crossed.

"Nung," shouted Tynan. Nung!''

"Yes.'' The man appeared at Tynan's side as if he were a ghost.

"Spread the men out along this bank. Two lines. One just inside the trees, and when the NVA try to cross, hose them down. Then we fall back, let the second line open fire, and while Charlie is pondering that, we all split for South Vietnam.''

"I no go to South Vietnam. I no live there.''

"Don't worry about it. Once we're there, I can get us some artillery or air support and helicopters to lift us out. Then they'll fly you into your village.''

"I—''

"Get the men organized. We don't have much time.''

While Nung positioned his men, Tynan studied his map. It looked as if they were within ten or twelve miles of the border, probably just outside of artillery range. He jammed the map into his pocket and turned.

Nung had the men divided. Those closest to the bank were concealed well, waiting for the enemy. Tynan leaped out, into the center of the stream, the water cold and refreshing. He could see evidence of their crossing in the mud and silt stirred up in the slow moving water. Then, from the opposite of the stream, hidden by the depths of the jungle, Tynan heard the enemy. A hundred soldiers not concerned with noise discipline. He could hear them shouting at one another, hear the rattling of their equipment as they ran.

"Nung, tell your men not to fire until I do. Let me start the shooting."

Nung spoke to them quietly, rapidly, and then whispered, "They wait for you."

Across the stream, a single NVA soldier appeared. He stopped, looked at the footprints on the bank, looked at the water that was slowly clearing. He crouched, reached out with his hand as if he didn't believe it was water.

Under his breath, Tynan said, "Don't anyone shoot him. Don't shoot him."

The man looked up at the jungle where Tynan and his men were hidden and then got to his feet. He turned and ran back into the jungle. A second later a squad approached. They stopped on the bank, looked to the rear, and began to ford the stream. Twenty men joined them.

At that instant, Tynan opened fire, pulling the trigger as fast as he could. The men with him opened fire and the front rank of enemy soldiers fell, their blood staining the water. There was shouting and a bugle call. The NVA soldiers shot back as they retreated.

Tynan was on his feet. "Nung! Get them out of here! Let's go."

The men, without a word from Nung, scrambled from their places, racing into the jungle, past their friends. Tynan halted with the second line. "Nung. Tell them to wait for me. Tell them not to shoot until I do."

As Nung rattled off the instruction, Tynan spun and crouched behind a large tree. He jerked the magazine from his weapon and reloaded. Then he turned, looking at the stream. There were five or six bodies in it, their blood turning it a crimson that looked like the reflection from a dying sun. More of them lay on the bank, their bodies missing hands or legs. Their weapons and equipment were scattered around them.

Tynan watched but the enemy didn't reappear. He wondered if they had forced them to retreat and then realized what was happening.

"Nung! Let's get out of here. Now! Move it!"

Together they got the men on their feet and running. Running deeper into the jungle, following the point man as he ran straight for South Vietnam. Running for the safety that the distance would give them.

From the rear he heard a shout and a burst of firing as the NVA assaulted their former position from the flank. Tynan had thought that they would try another frontal assault and then realized that the NVA would try to outflank him. He had gotten his men out of the way just in time.

Tynan kept running. He pushed past a couple of the strikers. They didn't have time to plan anymore because the enemy was too close to them. They could only run, hoping that the NVA would be a little more cautious after the ambush. That they would slow the pursuit because they didn't know where Tynan and the men might be hiding.

Tynan came to one man who was leaning against a tree, his weapon lying on the ground at his feet. He was breathing hard and sweating profusely. Tynan grabbed the shoulder straps of his rucksack, jerking him upright. Tynan scooped the man's rifle off the ground, handed it to him, and pushed him forward, making him run.

They kept running until their chests hurt and their lungs burned. They ran on feet that ached from the pounding and ran with cotton in their mouths. They ran with sweat dripping from them, making their hands slippery. They ran until they thought they would drop. And then they ran some more because each of them knew that stopping would be fatal. Stopping would let the NVA catch them, and there were now hundreds of the enemy chasing them.

They kept running until Tynan noticed that the men were slowing down, no longer able to keep up the pace. More of them were falling to the side, and Tynan was taking more of his time to help them up, to propel them forward.

Behind him, he could hear nothing. There was no shooting, there was no crashing like men running through a jungle. There was just an ominous silence, and Tynan wondered if the NVA had good radio communications. If that was the case, Tynan was sure that they were fucked. The leader of the pursuit might just have called someone else to cut off Tynan and his strikers. It's what he would do in South Vietnam if the situation was reversed.

There was nothing he could do about that. He needed to keep moving. Keep running. Keep the men moving, running toward South Vietnam.

And then he ran right into Nung, who was crouched by a large bush, using his rifle to keep from slumping over, his breath rasping in his throat.

Tynan stopped near him and wiped the sweat from his forehead.

He looked at his hand and then rubbed it against his thigh, leaving a ragged stain there.

"We've got to move," said Tynan. "We can't stop yet."

"Must," said Nung. "Can't go on."

"Then we'll die. We have to get out of here before the enemy catches us."

"Too late," gasped Nung. "NVA all around us."

"What the fuck are you talking about?"

"NVA soldiers in front of us. Moving down highway. Too many for us to fight."

Tynan looked up and turned toward the east, not understanding. How had the NVA gotten in front of them? And then, without Nung saying another word, he understood. They had run all the way to the Ho Chi Minh Trail and trapped themselves. Trapped themselves as surely as if they had painted themselves into a corner.

13

Tynan hesitated for just a moment. There was still no sign of a pursuit from the rear, but the enemy had to be there. He followed Nung through the jungle until they came out on a small ridge, concealed from the people below them by the trees and the bushes. He crawled forward and looked down at a small stretch of the Ho Chi Minh Trail that was bathed in the last of the light from the dying sun.

"Jesus Christ," he said. "All they need is the fucking stripe down the center and they've got a highway."

Nung looked at him but said nothing.

Tynan was watching the truck that was weaving in and out among the men with bicycles with bundles strapped to them. Two columns of soldiers walked down either side of the road. Every man carried some kind of weapon. Most of them had either AK-47s or SKS's, although more than one had an RPG-7.

Tynan turned so that he could see back the way they had just come. Still there was nothing behind him. No noise. No shouting. Just the ominous sounds from the jungle. He twisted around and stared at the trail.

The one thing that struck him was the impression that he had always had about it as a path through deep jungle, hidden there so that American fighters and bombers wouldn't be able to disrupt the flow of supplies to the south. But this was a highway. It looked as if it was made of concrete because of the gray color. He didn't think that it had been paved, but he was no longer sure of anything.

He did know that there was no way to sneak around it. It stretched far to the north with various branches that broke off to different points in North Vietnam. And it continued to the south, into Cambodia, finally terminating, according to some maps he had seen, in the Gulf of Siam. No way to circle around it. They had to cross it.

He glanced at Nung and said, "We wait for dark and hope the traffic slows down." Even as he said it, he knew that it wouldn't happen. If anything, the traffic would pick up during the night. Darkness was the ally of the men moving the supplies, protecting them from American jets.

And then, behind him, he heard the first sounds that the NVA were closing in. A command in Vietnamese. He didn't know what was meant, or why it was shouted, but he did hear it. The pursuit hadn't been abandoned.

"Fuck," he said. His vocabulary was disintegrating rapidly under the pressure of the moment.

He glanced at Nung, the three men near him, the trail, and the jungle behind him. There was no longer any time. He had to make a decision. He had to do something. Or prepare for his last stand. He wondered if this was how Custer felt when he realized that all the Indians in the free world were about to swoop in on him.

He held up a hand as if to stop anyone from talking and said quietly, "Okay. Okay. I don't think the guys on the trail know we're here. If we burst out of the jungle shooting, we can probably get across."

Nung waited for more.

"We rush across like on the attack and keep right on going. Through the jungle. It's the only way."

"We go now?"

"Yeah, we better fucking go now," said Tynan. "Get the men down the slope to the edge of the trail. Wait for my command and then run across it shooting."

"I understand."

"Then let's go."

Tynan moved away from the edge of the ridge, slipped to the right where the vegetation was thicker, providing more cover. He started down, dodged farther to the right, and then dropped four feet to the level ground. He leaped over a fallen tree and found himself staring at the Ho Chi Minh Trail. It wasn't paved with concrete, but had been covered with pea gravel. He could tell that the surface was smooth, probably compressed by millions of feet, thousands of loaded bicycles, and hundreds of trucks. It was an impressive engineering feat, and Tynan wished that he could admire it in color photographs while sitting in Washington rather than standing in the jungle inches away from it.

Within minutes the remainder of his tiny force joined him. He thought that he had lost the pursuers, and then heard them behind him, still up on the ridge, but closing in. He knew that he could wait no longer. Nung was crouched beside him, his rifle held at the ready. Tynan worked the bolt to make sure that a round was chambered. He ejected a good one and let it fall to the jungle floor.

"Let's go," he shouted and leaped out. He fired from the hip. There was a man with a bike to the left. Tynan shot at him, saw the bullets strike him and knock him over his bike. The man's feet tangled in the bike as he rolled over. He clawed at his chest and tried to sit up but didn't make it.

Firing broke out around him. The walking men dived for cover, some of them trying to unsling their weapons. There was a ripple of shots and a single explosion as a grenade went off.

Tynan sprinted across the trail, saw one of the VC in front of him, and fired. The round hit the man in the chin and flipped him back. Blood spurted, staining his uniform and the ground near him.

A second soldier spun, his weapon coming up. Tynan swung his, the barrel smashing into the NVA's. Tynan snapped the butt up and around, connecting with the soldier's face. He heard the bones in the face break as the man collapsed with a shriek of pain, his hands to his head.

Tynan pushed forward, saw another soldier, and fired twice, both rounds punching into the enemy's stomach. The man threw his rifle out in front of him and fell forward, putting out his hands. He hit the ground without a sound.

Now there was firing all around him. AKs against the M-1s of the strikers. Loud, single shots, and quieter bursts sounding like the ripping of cloth. Another grenade detonated somewhere behind them.

Tynan spun, facing the trail again. Through the gaps in the vegetation, he could see several bodies lying on the pea gravel. A couple of them were strikers, cut down by the NVA. Tynan saw one of them try to get up as another round hit him. He screamed with a sound like tires on dry concrete, and died.

The firing was tapering off as the strikers punched through the NVA on the trail. Tynan hesitated and then started forward again. Nung was in front of him and two strikers were far ahead of both of them.

Tynan wanted to shout at them, urge them to run faster. He could feel the excitement bubbling in his chest. He felt a desire to scream, to shout, caused by the pumping of the adrenaline, but he ignored it. He ran harder, leaping over a small bush, and swinging his rifle to clear the vines from his path.

There was still distant shooting and Tynan didn't know if it was the enemy firing at shadows, or if some of the strikers had failed to break through. He was tempted to go back to check, but knew that would be fatal. He had to keep moving forward, fleeing toward South Vietnam. Deep inside he felt that he was betraying the strikers, running out on them. It wasn't true, because each of the men understood the plan. And then he realized that he didn't know what the strikers thought. He didn't know if they understood the plan. The idea had been filtered through a third party, and Tynan didn't know what he had said.

But that didn't stop him. There was no way that he could stop. He had to keep running for the sanctuary of the Vietnamese border, the line on the ground where he could gain artillery support and close air support, and maybe even find a company of American soldiers who would delight at the chance to shoot holes in the enemy.

Around him were the remnants of the striker force

that he had led away from Giap's headquarters. Up in front, a vague shadow now that night was nearly on them, was Nung, running. He held his rifle at high port, and his head was swiveling back and forth as if searching for the enemy. Just behind him were two more men, both with their weapons held high. It didn't look like a rout. It just felt that way.

And suddenly they all stopped. Nung halted, dropped to a knee, and spun. Tynan caught him and saw the problem. They were on a rock cliff, the floor of the jungle fifteen or twenty feet below them. The face was sheer with few handholds or footholds. Four or five stunted bushes grew from cracks in the cliff's face.

"Get a muster," said Tynan.

Nung shrugged and said, "Muster?"

"Find out who's here. How many men have been lost. Find out what happened to them."

"Yes. I see."

"And get some pickets out," Tynan told him. "Men at the rear of the formation to listen for the enemy." But he didn't know these people. They had performed well in all the situations they had come up against. They didn't run as the VC and NVA assaulted their positions, they had excellent patrol discipline, and they obeyed orders quickly. But he didn't know them.

"We rest here ten minutes and then we find a way off this cliff. I'll be at the rear seeing if I can find out what's happening there."

Nung moved off carefully, talking to the men, finding out the answers to Tynan's questions.

Tynan watched him for a moment and then worked his way to the rear. He saw two men sitting with their backs to a tree, their weapons across their knees.

They looked physically exhausted. Tynan wondered how he could run them into the ground in their own country and then decided it must be the diet. He had eaten better than they did for years, and after two days of constant strain, it was beginning to show. It didn't mean that Tynan wasn't tired, or that he could run rings around them now. They just seemed to be showing the effects of the last two days a little more than he was.

He found the edge of his formation. Three men crouched under a large bush with big orange flowers on it. Tynan moved to the right and dropped behind a fallen palm. He listened carefully but heard nothing other than the normal noise as the monkeys swung through the trees and the birds called to one another. There was the chirp of insects and the buzz of flies as the sun disappeared. But there was nothing that sounded like a man trying to move silently.

For the first time since he left John with the sniper rifle and a half-baked idea of shooting Giap, Tynan had a chance to think about it. And he didn't like it. Didn't like leaving men behind and didn't like running from the NVA. In a stand-up fight, the NVA always came out on the short end, unless they had overwhelming numbers. Then they beat the Americans and the South Vietnamese, but only if they outnumbered the Americans by five or six to one.

It was like the Indian Wars in the Old West. The Indians never fought unless they chose the time and the place and had the numbers. The Army was forever chasing them and rarely catching them. And then Tynan remembered something else. The very last thing a soldier wanted to do was get into a running gun battle. It let the Indians whittle away at your force, cut it down slowly until it was too small to survive. And that was the situation Tynan found himself in. A running gun battle with the NVA and no safety until he reached the South Vietnamese border. He thought about what John had said just before Tynan had taken off. It was the same sort of thing. Of course, Tynan had a destination that was close now. All he had to do was cross the imaginary line and he had it made.

He pulled out his map and studied it in the last of the light. It was hard to tell exactly where they were. No landmarks other than a small stream they had crossed, and the Ho Chi Minh Trail which no one marked on maps and everyone pretended was some kind of nearly useless jungle path. The terrain markings showed a steep decline near him, but that was all it showed. No real clues. He could be five miles or ten miles from the border. Or nearly on top of it.

And then he heard the first sounds of the enemy. Their noise discipline was good, but not good enough. There was a rattling of metal. Tynan pulled back, to the large bush, touched the shoulder of one of the men and motioned him to retreat. He caught the attention of the other two, and they all fell back.

Nung was standing at the edge of the cliff looking down. When he saw Tynan, he moved closer to him. "I find twenty-four men. The others are not here."

"We lose anyone crossing the trail?"

"I do not know. I think two, maybe three men not make it. I just not know."

"Okay. Let's get out of here. Point man to scout along cliff until we find a way down. Then we head due east. Zero-nine-zero on the compass."

Behind him, the noise of the pursuit was growing. He understood that the NVA didn't have to worry about Tynan and his strikers attacking them and killing them. There weren't enough strikers and there were too many NVA, but there was something wrong. They were making too much noise and Tynan didn't like it. They were too tired for good noise discipline. But there was no time to worry about it. He had to get his men moving again.

The point man took off, running along the edge of the cliff where the vegetation was the lightest and thinnest. A squad of men followed him closely. Others joined in, straggling along in a confused dash away from the enemy. Nung was in the middle of that group. A last squad, only ten men, began to move then. Tynan joined them.

They continued along the top of the cliff for nearly a half klick and then found a gentle slope where the cliff joined a higher hill. Immediately the point man veered to his right, running down the hill. He halted at the bottom, and when the main body caught him he took off again.

They came to a trail, a very narrow path in the jungle that was partially overgrown by grass. Overhead branches from the taller trees formed a roof over the trail. Tynan didn't like using the trail but didn't stop them. It was now dark, and they couldn't fight their way through the jungle and keep the NVA behind them. They needed the trail to make some time.

They kept moving for an hour, slowing from a jog as the sun set to a rapid walk. Two men were on point, searching for pitfalls and obstacles, but not slowing. Finally the men were exhausted and Tynan had to call a halt, give them a chance to drink some water and eat some food. It was all the time they had.

Within ten minutes, Tynan had them on their feet

again. He had studied his map as best he could. He had draped his poncho over his head and used several of his matches, nearly setting it on fire. As near as he could tell, they were either in South Vietnam or damned close to it.

Tynan got them on their feet. It took him a while to do it. They didn't want to get up. They didn't want to move. Through Nung, Tynan told them that there were more NVA coming. Many more, and if they didn't get out of there, they would all die. Still, the men were reluctant to move until they all heard the sounds of the NVA searching for them.

Quietly, rapidly, the strikers began moving, heading to the east. Tyan waited to make sure that everyone had gotten up. He wanted to remain behind to search the ground for dropped equipment but couldn't take the time. All he could do was hope that John had drilled the strikers in the importance of not giving the NVA any help. He hoped they would keep all their equipment rather than throw it away at the first opportunity.

When it seemed that the NVA were no more than a few feet from him, he ran after the strikers, feeling like a lion being driven by the beaters during a hunting safari. He forced the thought from his mind and concentrated on catching the strikers and getting to South Vietnam.

Then, suddenly, he knew why he felt that he was running into a trap. There was a single explosion somewhere to the front, followed by the ripping noise of an RPD firing. A dozen AKs, a hundred, began firing, and through the breaks in the vegetation, Tynan could see the sparkling of the muzzle flashes popping like the strobes of a thousand cameras.

Tynan dived to the ground and waited, listening

and watching. His men began firing, their vintage weapons against the best the NVA and VC had. There were explosions from Chicom grenades as the ambushers tried to wipe them out. And in that moment, Tynan understood why the NVA had been so noisy. They had been driving them toward the ambush. It was a beautifully coordinated attack, and if Tynan hadn't been hugging the ground, his nose in the foul-smelling dirt of the jungle floor, he would have admired them.

14

For the first few moments, it seemed that the firefight would stabilize, with the NVA content to keep the trapped men right where they were. Tynan could hear the bullets tearing through the jungle above him, shredding the leaves of the bushes and trees, raining debris down on them. The firing from the enemy was steady, an almost rhythmic hammering of automatic weapons. It was the first time that Tynan had been aware of the sound of the firing as individual weapons. In the past, there had been noise, shouting and shooting and bugles, but not the hammering of the weapons.

He crawled forward slowly, inching his way toward the front of their position. He found the body of one of the strikers. He stopped long enough to see if he could help the man, but the wound was so massive—a bullet had torn into his shoulder and traveled downward to break bones and smash the heart—that Tynan knew the man was dead. He took the weapon and spare ammo and continued on.

He found Nung sitting upright next to a tiny bush

that offered him no protection. He had his hands wrapped around his thigh. There was a single small hole in it pouring blood. Nung's hands were on either side of his leg, but well away from the wound.

Tynan looked up into his eyes and saw that they were glassy with pain. Nung's face had gotten waxy-looking, and Tynan didn't know if it was from blood loss or shock. He tried to push Nung's hands out of the way so that he could bandage the wound, but Nung wouldn't cooperate. He sat there, his teeth clenched and his hands locked on his thigh.

Around him, the shooting was continuing. Tynan could still see some of the muzzle flashes and heard some outgoing rounds in response, but no one on either side seemed inclined to move. The NVA were obviously waiting for something now that they had the strikers pinned down.

Tynan forced Nung to lie back. He took the dressing from Nung's first aid kit, shook it out, and prepared to tie it around the wounded man's leg. Nung suddenly jerked away, sat up again, and screamed something unintelligible. Then he sank to the jungle floor, kicked his foot, and died.

Again, Tynan stripped the dead man of his weapon and ammo. He glanced at Nung's face and wondered how he was going to talk to the strikers now. He was surrounded by friendly soldiers and didn't know one word of their language. He shrugged, wondered if there was something he should say about the dead man, and then continued to the perimeter.

Once there, he learned that the strikers were only shooting when they had a target. John had taught them everything, including fire discipline. They seemed to realize that they had only limited amounts of ammo and they shouldn't just burn it up. They had to conserve it until the NVA launched a real attack against them.

Tynan found himself a good position at the base of a teak tree with roots that branched out around him, giving him a slight depression in which to crouch. The thick roots also gave him some protection from bullets and shrapnel. He made sure they were loaded and then set the two rifles, another M-1 carbine, and a Garand behind him, out of the way. He arranged it so that he could grab either one quickly.

Finally sure that his position was momentarily secure, Tynan took out his map, but in the dark he couldn't see it. He stretched his poncho liner over his head, making sure that it reached the ground. He didn't like doing that with the shooting going on around him, but the NVA hadn't rushed them yet and he had to know where he was. If he could pinpoint his coordinates, he might be able to get some help from the artillery bases nearby. He studied the map quickly in the dim, flickering light of his last matches and thought that he had a good fix on his position. He memorized the coordinates and then whipped the poncho off his head.

Before he could act on the information there was a single shout in Vietnamese and the enemy came rushing out of the jungle at them. Tynan lifted his rifle but didn't use the sights. He aimed by looking over the top of the barrel and pulled the trigger rapidly. He saw one shadowy soldier topple, but another took his place. Tynan managed to shoot him, and then the NVA were running past him, into the perimeter.

A lone man loomed out of the blackness directly in front of him. Tynan fell back, against the trunk of the tree, braced the butt of his rifle there, and fired from the hip. The man turned, raised his AK, and pulled the trigger. The burst was high, ripping into the tree over Tynan's head. He could feel the bullets smashing into the trunk.

Tynan fired again, three quick shots. The flame from the barrel seemed to leap out into the darkness like a beam of light. The tip of the flashes almost touched the shirt of the enemy soldier, and in the strobelike effect, Tynan saw blood stain the NVA's uniform. The man fell forward, collapsing into the depression.

As that happened, another enemy soldier leaped at him, swinging at his head with a machete. Tynan ducked under the blade and as the man tried to smash it downward to cleave Tynan's skull, Tynan swung the butt of his rifle around. He hit the man in the side of the head. The man fell and Tynan shot him once in the chest, the barrel of the rifle nearly touching him.

Out of the corner of his eye, he saw someone running toward him. Tynan fired a couple of shots, but the man didn't stop. Tynan dropped to his knee, aimed, and fired again. The man threw his weapon upward, over his head. He stumbled and seemed to claw at the air, trying to gain his balance. He fell to the ground with a grunt and didn't move.

All around him, Tynan was aware of the battle. There was the scrape of metal against metal. There were grunts and cries from the men. Single shots and short bursts. He stared into the night, caught flashes as the men fired their weapons.

He turned, put his back against the tree, and watched for the enemy. A soldier ran by him, but Tynan didn't have a chance to react. He spun but before he could get off a shot, the man had disappeared into the jungle.

And then it seemed that the VC and NVA were running by him in the other direction. The shooting seemed to increase as the two sides separated. Tynan fired at several of the enemy soldiers but didn't hit any of them.

The firing between the two sides increased then. The RPD opened fire again, trying to suppress the strikers, its green tracers flashing into the jungle around him. Tynan searched the trees, but the NVA had it well hidden and he couldn't see the muzzle flashes.

As the attack broke, Tynan fell to his knees. He reloaded his weapon and then set it to the side. He took the tiny survival radio from his pack and pulled out the antenna. That activiated it, and he heard the carrier wave clearly. He turned down the volume and whispered into it. "Any arty advisory, any arty advisory, this is Deathstalker Six."

He waited for a moment and then repeated his message. There was a burst of static and then a voice said, "Deathstalker Six, this is Dak Sut arty. Go ahead."

"Roger. This is Deathstalker Six with a fire mission."

"Understand fire mission."

"Roger. We have a possible NVA company attacking in jungle at Grid Yankee Bravo six-five-four-nine. Area fire and quick fuse."

There was a moment's hesitation and then, "Please check coordinates again. Be advised that location is not in South Vietnam."

"Coordinates are correct," said Tynan.

"Is the enemy close to you?"

"Hang on for a moment and I'll let you talk to them."

"Deathstalker Six, can you authenticate?"

"Dak Sut arty, I can try. Authentication table six."

"I have two-one-one-seven."

"Four-eight-six-three," said Tynan.

"Marking round on the way," was the response.

Tynan waited, looking for the white phosphorus explosion that was the smoke round. He listened for the telltale noise of the artillery round but didn't hear it. The firing around him continued.

Finally he had to say something. He took a guess and said, "Add three hundred and right three hundred."

"Shot over."

"Shot out," said Tynan as he waited. A moment later he caught a dim flash in the jungle. The rumble of the explosion finally drifted to him like thunder in the late afternoon.

"Right five hundred. Add three hundred."

"Deathstalker Six, be advised that your coordinates are nearly a klick off."

"Roger," snapped Tynan. He was going to explain that it was hard to read a map at night with the enemy around you, shooting at you with everything they owned, but didn't. Instead, he said, "Understood shot?"

"Roger, shot, over."

Tynan didn't repeat that time. Instead he ducked as the artillery round detonated a hundred meters in front of him. He keyed the mike and nearly shouted, "Right on. Fire for effect."

"Rounds on the way."

"Roger." Tynan dropped into the bottom of the depression, closing his eyes and waiting. There was a harsh whoosh and then a series of explosions. Tynan could hear the shrapnel spinning through the jungle. There were screams from the enemy lines and the small-arms fire tapered off.

There were six explosions, a hesitation, and six more. The radio crackled to life. "Please advise."

"Keep it coming," yelled Tynan. "Pour it on."

"Rounds on the way."

Tynan listened to the explosions as the artillery ripped through the jungle. The area in front of them was saturated by the artillery. Anyone in there had to be dead, or had to have run away. As he thought about it, he realized that it might be the way to get out of the box. Call off the artillery, attack through the NVA position while they had their heads down waiting for the next barrage, and then call it in again, letting it close off the pursuit.

"Last rounds on the way," said the man.

"Roger." Tynan was on his feet. He grabbed the weapons he had with him and ran to the right. He found one of the strikers and yelled at him, "You speak English?"

"No. No."

There was another man close and Tynan pointed at him. "You. You speak English?"

"Little."

"We go." said Tynan. "That way."

"No."

"Yes." He dropped as the last six rounds hit. "Now! Get everybody. We must run."

The man stared at him and then shouted something. Tynan didn't like that, but with all the noise from the artillery and the sporadic firing, he didn't see how it could hurt.

Then, before he did anything else, he stripped the bolts from the weapons he had taken off the dead men. He stuffed those in his pack, figuring that he would be disabling the weapons for a while. It wasn't like leaving a whole one for the enemy.

Then as he saw the men gathering he said, "We run. Follow me."

He pushed around a bush and jogged forward, waiting for the RPD to open fire, but that didn't happen. Suddenly he was among the broken, smoking trees where the artillery had landed. There were several small fires burning, and in the overturned, bare earth, he could see a couple of bodies. He didn't stop. He kept moving, jumping over the damaged trees, leaping around the remains of a bunker that had taken a direct hit, and then found himself in jungle that hadn't been shelled. He kept running, glancing right and left, and saw that the strikers were still with him, running right beside him.

Tynan stopped then and waved at the men. "Keep moving. Keep moving." He jerked out the antenna of the radio and said, "Dak Sut arty. Resume fire mission, same coordinates."

"Can you spot?"

"Negative."

"Roger. Rounds on the way."

Tynan used the palm of his hand to telescope the antenna into the radio. He then began to run again, following the strikers. He heard the artillery rumble overhead and then saw the flashes of the explosions out of the corner of his eye. He was tempted to stop, watch the cannon cockers do their thing, and see if there was any sign of a pursuit, but he didn't. He just ran, following the strikers, feeling that he had betrayed John and the men who had died and Boone and Sterne and even Jones—Jones, who was lying wounded in some unmarked village.

The mission had been a boondoggle from the moment he had stepped into Walker's office and now it seemed that everyone on it was dead, or about to die. He had left men scattered all over Laos. Left them to the VC and the NVA while he continued to run, always in the direction of safety. Just because it was the way the mission was breaking didn't make it any easier. Nor did the fact that it seemed that the mission was a waste of time and lives.

Tynan forced the thoughts from his mind because there were other things he had to worry about. He had to guess how far it was to the South Vietnamese border. He knew he had to be close or the artillery would have never been cleared to fire in support. And he had to worry about how to convince the military to send in choppers to pick them up. And he had to worry about staying alive until all that could happen, because he wanted to see Walker and his CIA cronies again. Wanted to see them badly.

But at that moment all he could do was continue to run. Continue to head to the east, being careful that he didn't run off a cliff or into another ambush or a booby trap. Just continue to move until it was morning and they were in South Vietnam. Then he would have all day to figure something out.

It was an hour before dawn when they stopped. They ran out of the jungle and into a clearing that was two or three klicks across. It was on top of a gentle hill. The peak was in the open, sloping away to give them a clear killing field for five hundred meters in all directions. There was no source of water and no way to get off it if the VC surrounded them, but then Tynan didn't plan to escape and evade. He planned on helicopters landing to pluck them out of danger.

He grabbed the man who could speak a little English and said, "We stay here."

"Here?" repeated the man.

"Right here. I want pickets in the trees to the west. Two men to a position here. Dig in and prepare to repel an assault."

The man stood there just looking dumb. He had one hand on his hip as he sucked in his breath. "Here?"

"Okay," said Tynan. "Have the men dug in. Two men right here." Tynan pointed to the ground. "Dig in." He moved to the left, pointed at the shallow depression, and added, "Two men here. You see?"

"We make circle."

"Yeah, a circle. Let's get it done."

The man started shouting instructions in his native language. Tynan understood why the American Army was having all the trouble with the Vietnamese. Not only did they have to train them how to fight, they needed to use interpreters, and who knew how the message was screwed up in all the translations?

He watched as the man deployed the strikers. In five minutes he had them digging shallow holes that could be fighting positions if the VC or NVA found them. Tynan moved to the center and dug his own hole.

It was beginning to lighten when he finished. The black of the sky was changing to gray. He watched as the stars faded and a red glow crept higher until he could see the ground around him. The trees in the jungle were still black shapes but they were beginning to take form. He pulled out his map, studied it, and tried to figure out where they were.

He sat back, leaning on the crumbling dirt of his hole, his head resting against the rotting log he had pulled closer. He took out his radio, jerked the antenna into position, and said clearly, "Mayday, Mayday, Mayday. This is Deathstalker Six on the ground south of Dak Sut and west of Dak To. Mayday, Mayday, Mayday."

"Deathstalker Six, this is Blackhawk One-Two. Say nature of emergency."

"Roger. I have a company of strikers on the ground. We have been badly mauled by the NVA. Need airlift out."

"Are you in contact?"

"Negative. We have broken contact. Have secured suitable landing zone. Require nine helos."

"Understood. Stand by."

Tynan collapsed the antenna and then realized that shut off the radio. He pulled the antenna out and set the radio on the ground by the log. He checked his rifle, changed the magazine, and then counted the number of magazines left. He had plenty of ammo. Running out was the least of his problems.

He closed his eyes and realized just how tired he was. He hadn't had any sleep since the hour or so he had caught the morning before. Since that time he had run a long way, been involved in a couple of firefights, and watched a lot of people die. The adrenaline had kept him going for a long time, but now that high was wearing off. He wanted to sleep. He thought that he would let the others worry about pickets and guards and then remembered that there was no one around him to do it. If he didn't take care of the problem, no one would.

He forced himself to sit up. He dropped his pack and stood, his rifle held in one hand. From where he stood, he could see that most of the men had finished digging their holes. They had been well placed, but that had been easy. They had no heavy weapons left, so he didn't have to worry about placing the machine guns so that they could support each other. All they really had to do was sit tight and wait for the helicopters.

A single shot from an AK-47 rang out. Tynan dropped to the ground, crawled to his hole, and yelled, ''Anyone see where that came from?''

No one answered.

And then it wasn't important. They attack came without any more warning. The NVA and VC swarmed out of the trees, running silently over the broken ground of the clearing. They were nearly halfway to the foxholes when the first shots were fired by the strikers. One of the men began dropping M-79 rounds in the middle of the oncoming enemy. Small black clouds of smoke and dust billowed. Soldiers fell, but the majority kept coming.

Tynan fired his rifle, picking his targets carefully. He saw the dirt fly off the uniforms as the bullets struck and the men died. He emptied his rifle, snapped a fresh magazine in, and searched for another target.

But the firing from the strikers wasn't heavy enough. The NVA, trained in human wave assault and hyped on drugs, rushed into the onslaught of firing. They didn't waver or falter. They came on, shouting suddenly, as if someone had thrown a switch. They were screaming in rage and they began firing their weapons.

The shooting seemed to taper as the NVA reached the line of foxholes. The strikers leaped to meet them, using their bayonets, pistols, and knives.

Tynan waited in a crouch, firing as he identified the enemy shapes. The NVA were so mixed with the strikers that it was hard to shoot without endangering his own men. One of the enemy separated from the group, penetrated the defensive line, and ran at Tynan with his head down, bayonet extended. Tynan aimed and fired. The man fell to the ground, rolled, and was still.

In front of him, he saw one of the strikers struggling with an NVA soldier. The striker flipped the enemy, dropped on his chest with a knee, and stabbed the soldier. As he turned, another enemy thrust once, catching the striker in the stomach with a bayonet. The striker grabbed the rifle, twisted and pulled it from the enemy's hands. He then killed the NVA before he collapsed.

Tynan fired again as more of the NVA broke through. He killed two of them. He spun, saw another, but before he could fire, someone leaped at him, knocking him to the ground. Tynan lost the grip on his rifle. He rolled to the side and jerked his combat knife free. The NVA came at him, bayonet out. Tynan grabbed the barrel of the weapon, pulled it hard, and then slashed at the throat of the enemy. There was a momentary resistance as the knife sliced the tender skin of the enemy's neck. Blood spurted, washing down the front of his uniform. The NVA dropped his rifle, raised his hands, but then fell forward, dying.

Another man came at Tynan. He spun, caught the man's arm, and swung his hip into him. He flipped the enemy, punched him in the face, and then plunged the knife into his chest just under the breastbone.

He heard the radio burst into life. The helicopter pilot was asking for information, but Tynan didn't have the time to provide it. He saw another of the NVA running at him. Tynan dropped his knife and grabbed one of the AKs. He worked the bolt and aimed. He fired quickly, killing two of the NVA soldiers.

He spun, saw another, and shot him. He looked around, but it seemed that the NVA had fled. He could see one or two running for the cover of the trees. Scattered in front of him were the bodies of fifty or sixty men, many of them in the dark green of the NVA, but quite a few of them in the fatigues of the strikers. He could hear moaning from the field. He saw a couple of men moving, trying to help the wounded.

Tynan grabbed the radio and yelled, "Blackhawk One-Two, this is Deathstalker Six. We are under attack. I repeat. Under attack."

"Roger Six," came the calm voice of the pilot. "Say location of the enemy."

"To the southwest of our position, in the trees."

"Can you throw smoke?" asked the pilot.

"Negative. I have no smoke."

"Do you have us in sight?" asked the pilot.

"Negative."

"Roger. We should be over your location in zero five minutes. We will have gunship support. Please spot for us."

"Understood." Tynan looked to the east, where the sun had risen above the horizon. In the distance, he saw a black speck that could have been a helicopter. "I have you in sight," said Tynan. "You are due east of our location."

"Roger. We are inbound. Keep your heads down."

Tynan waited as the helicopters approached. When they were nearly overhead, he radioed, "The NVA position is to the southwest."

"Roger. We see the line of bodies."

At that moment, one of the gunships rolled in firing rockets. There were twin whooshes from it and twin explosions in the trees. The jungle erupted, green tracers lancing upward, toward the helicopter. There was a steady chugging as a .51-caliber machine gun began to shoot.

The lead helicopter broke to the right as the next one rolled in. There was a loud, long buzz as the miniguns fired into the jungle. Tynan watched as it seemed that a red ray danced over the jungle canopy, but the heavy machine gun fell silent and the number of green tracers flying upward declined.

"Deathstalker Six. Can you authenticate?"

"Roger."

They went through the procedure quickly. Then Blackhawk One-Two said, "We have a flight of slicks inbound. Be prepared to load in two minutes."

Tynan rogered and then wondered if John had ever drilled the men on helicopter operations. He didn't know how they would react when the flight dropped on them. He hoped that they realized it was a way out. He crawled forward, looking for the one man who spoke English, but couldn't find him before he heard the helicopters coming in.

At that moment, the gunships began more runs, firing everything they had. Tynan saw the slicks, just above the trees, flying straight for the top of the hill. The NVA began shooting, their tracers crisscrossing with the ruby ones of the M-60 machine guns on the choppers. The sound of the firing was lost in the roar of the turbines and the beat of the rotor blades.

The flight didn't seem to slow, racing out of the sun. They all flared at the same moment, hauling their noses up and dropping their tails. Clouds of dust, grass, leaves, and debris were caught in the rotorwash and blown across the hill. As the skids of the helicopters touched the ground, the NVA began dropping mortars into the clearing.

Tynan was on his feet then, running for the first chopper. He leaped up, into the cargo compartment. He caught hold of the troop seat and pulled himself in. He turned, saw three of the strikers running at him. He moved back, leaned out, and waved them forward.

"Come on!" he shouted. "Come on!"

He saw others running across the open ground. The door guns of the Hueys were hammering, their tracers cutting into the jungle. The gunships kept pounding the NVA position, rockets flashing into it, exploding into balls of fire and clouds of shrapnel.

Then, suddenly, the aircraft was lifting off. The skids broke ground and the nose dumped. They raced forward, gaining speed until the pilot hauled back on the cyclic. The chopper climbed upward, the door guns still firing, until the clearing was left behind. Tynan saw the gunships circling well to the south.

He glanced at the strikers in the chopper with them. A couple were grinning, enjoying the ride and the sudden knowledge that they were going to live. Another clung to the troop seat, his eyes squeezed shut, looking as if he was about to be sick.

The crew chief leaned around the transmission and grinned at Tynan. He held a thumb up, telling Tynan they were clear. Telling him they were on their way back. Tynan grinned at the man, and wondered just what the hell had happened.

15

Within twelve hours of the helicopter's landing under fire in the mountain meadow, Tynan was in Cholon at the CIA building. He had slept on the helicopter from Dak Suk to Ban Me Thuot and then on the plane from Ban Me Thuot to Saigon. He was picked up at Tan Son Nhut and driven to Cholon, and had nearly fallen asleep in the jeep. On the way, he protested that he hadn't eaten anything but C-rations for the last several days, and he had eaten the last of those a day earlier. He was told not to worry, something would be ordered for him.

Once inside the building, he was taken down the same corridor, but instead of entering the office that guarded the theaterlike briefing room, he was taken around a corner to a conference room. Inside was a table of polished teak, six high-backed brown chairs, a small screen and slide projector, and a table that held a water pitcher and six glasses.

The Army sergeant who had escorted him said, "Have a seat and someone will join you in a moment. We'll have some food in here for you shortly. What would you like to drink?''

''A Coke, if you can scare up a cold one. If not, a beer, and failing that, anything that is wet.''

''Yes, sir. I'll see what I can do.''

Tynan rocked back in the chair and closed his eyes. He rubbed a hand over his face, feeling the stubble from his beard. They had given him time to shower at Dak Sut but not time to shave. They had even found a clean uniform for him. His old one was soaked with sweat, covered with mud, and torn in a dozen places. Once he had showered and changed, they had herded him to the helipad where the chopper waited, its blades spinning and its engine roaring.

It had been a real lousy mission. Dead men spread from South Vietnam to Laos, and he had no idea if it had been worth it. He had succeeded in killing a couple of NVA officers but knew that a blow like that to the American Army could be recovered in a matter of minutes. Hell, at Iwo Jima in World War II, command of some line companies had devolved to PFCs, and the units, though woefully undermanned, had stayed in the fight.

The door behind him opened and Tynan opened his eyes. Three men came in, two in civilian clothes and the third in uniform. The civilians were both tanned, about six feet tall, and healthy-looking. One was blond and the other had dark hair. If it hadn't been for the hair color, they would have been interchangable. Both had faces that seemed average. Eyes, noses, and mouths looked average.

The military man was a major who wore heavily starched fatigues that looked fresh. He was a stocky man with black hair, small, bright eyes, and a scar that ran from the point of his chin, up his cheek, and across the eyelid to disappear in his hair line. It was an impressive scar that looked to be only a few months old.

The men sat down on the side of the table opposite Tynan. The blond civilian said, "Well, Lieutenant. That was sure a fucked-up mission."

Tynan leaned forward, his elbows on the table, and asked, "Are you suggesting that it was somehow my fault?"

"You were in command and only you returned," said the blond.

"Are you implying something by that?" asked Tynan, the anger umistakable in his voice.

"Oh no," said the dark-haired man. "I think that Jason here was merely making an observation. Why don't you fill us in on your activities during the last few days?"

Tynan took a deep breath and let it out slowly. He hesitated, looking into the eyes of each of the men facing him, wondering just what the hell was going on. Then he began talking about the mission, mentioning that the briefing had been conducted in this building. Before he had gotten far into his narrative, the food arrived and was set before him. He picked up the Coke, drank half of it and asked for a refill.

The men watched him eat for a few minutes, until he had taken the edge off his hunger, and then asked him to continue. Around forkfuls of steak or baked potato or peas, he told them, in detail, about the mission once they had touched down in Laos. About the ambush that killed two of his men and wounded another. About heading for the CIA-financed and controlled village and the agent there who suggested that they continue.

The blond interrupted and asked, "The man tell you he was a CIA agent?"

"No," said Tynan quickly, remembering that John had finally confessed that he worked for the CIA. "Just said he worked for the government and seemed to know exactly what I was there for. I just assumed that he was a CIA man."

"Don't go making those assumptions too far afield," said the dark-haired man. "It wouldn't be a good idea for too many people to realize that there are Americans in Laos training the locals in guerrilla warfare."

"I hadn't planned on mentioning it outside this room," said Tynan.

"Oh."

He told them about spliting into two teams, Geist leading one, while he and the assumed CIA man led the other. At that point, Tynan asked, "What's happened to Geist?" He'd asked before, but no one ever had an answer.

"Sergeant Geist is still in the field, as far as we can determine," said the blond.

"As far as you can determine?" repeated Tynan.

"Let's just say that we have information that he took out the commanding officer of an NVA division yesterday."

"You've got some excellent sources," said Tynan sarcastically.

"Yes, we do."

Tynan then told them about infiltrating the town, the opportunity to take out a couple of ranking officers, and the running gun battle to get clear.

"That would have been Ban Vin," said the dark man.

"If you say so. Our map didn't name the town, though it was fairly large."

Tynan continued his narration as he finished the last of the steak and potatoes. It was the best meal he had eaten while in Vietnam, and he wondered why the common grunt in the field never got to eat that well.

As he put down his fork, he said, "The last I saw of John, he was trying to climb a tree to get a shot at Giap. I don't suppose that he succeeded?"

"We have no information on that. John, as you call him, has failed to make his weekly report, but given the circumstances, there is no reason for concern at this point. As far as we can determine, General Giap has returned to the North."

Tynan reached for the Coke but his hand stopped halfway there. "You have information that Giap returned North?"

"It is an unsubstantiated report, but that is the information."

"Then that would mean that the planned invasion is off," said Tynan slowly, thinking as he spoke. "They would want their hero of Dien Bien Phu to lead this invasion."

The military man spoke for the first time. "That is the way that we see it."

"Then the mission wasn't just an exercise in futility," said Tynan. He looked at each of the men and said, "How many teams did you have out?"

The blond shrugged. "Obviously enough."

Tynan rocked back in his chair, the Coke forgotten on the table. He didn't know exactly what he felt. A thrill that the deaths of his men weren't a waste. Satisfaction that the mission had been well done after all. A feeling that he hadn't betrayed the men who had died. Or maybe an anger that these men had come into the conference pretending that Tynan had somehow failed.

"The buildup has stopped?" asked Tynan quietly.

"Some of the units have been dispersed. One has returned to the North. Traffic on the Ho Chi Minh Trail has slowed significantly in the last two days. Intelligence reports also indicate a dispersal of the VC units along all the border areas in South Vietnam."

"Say, you know what that trail looks like?" asked Tynan suddenly. As he spoke, he realized that his mind was running wild. He was having trouble concentrating and knew that it was a lack of sleep. And the sudden lifting of the strain he had been under. He shook himself and said, "It's a fucking highway."

"We know. We have pictures."

"Okay," said Tynan. "Then I have a couple of questions for you. First, no one will tell me about Jones. I had to leave him in the village."

"Your fellow seaman has been evacuated to Da Nang. As soon as we learned where he was, we put an aircraft in to recover him. That same aircraft ferried the remainder of your strike force to their camp."

"How long we been doing this?" asked Tynan.

"You are now into an area where you have no need to know," said the dark-haired man quietly. "In fact, just forget about the villages in Laos. We have no one there working with the indigenous populations."

The blond man stood up and said, "I think we have everything we need." He glanced at the other two men. "Either of you have any questions?"

When each of them shook his head, the blond said, "We'll arrange transport for you back to Tan Son Nhut. If anything else comes up, we'll be in touch. Otherwise, please remember that this debriefing, and everything that you learned in the course of the mission, is classified. You are not at liberty to discuss it with anyone." The man smiled. "That includes your Commander Walker. Is that clear?"

"Perfectly."

The three men moved to the door without another word. Once the two civilians were gone, the military man looked back. "If it's any consolation, I know what it's like to lose men in combat. I doubt that you'll ever understand the value of your mission. It was a big help. You can bank on that. Now, just hang loose and someone will escort you to Tan Son Nhut.

A day later, Tynan sat in the rooftop restaurant of the Continental Hotel. Bobbi Harris sat across from him wearing a low-cut dress that revealed more than it covered. His eyes kept falling to the beads of sweat visible between her breasts. She smiled at him but said little.

Tynan drank his beer slowly, watching the traffic in the street below him. There were cars, trucks, jeeps and lambrettas. There were bicycles and motorcycles. And people. Thousands of people, circulating through the city, trying to separate the soldier, both American and Vietnamese, from his money. Hustles of every kind. Having just come from the jungle, Tynan thought it seemed all the more corrupt.

Tynan tore his eyes away from it and looked at Bobbi again. "You want to eat?"

"Not unless you're hungry," she said. "I had a big breakfast."

"Then let's see if we can find something better to do with our time."

She reached across the table and took his hand. As she stood up, she smiled deeply and said, "By all means."